CLUELESS™

ONE LAST SUMMER

BOOM! BOX™

For information regarding the CPSIA on this printed material, call: (203) 595-3636 and provide #RICH– 816413

BOOM! Studios, 5670 Wilshire Boulevard, Suite 400, Los Angeles, CA 90036-5679. Printed in USA. First Printing.

ISBN: 978-1-68415-259-9, eISBN: 978-1-64144-275-6

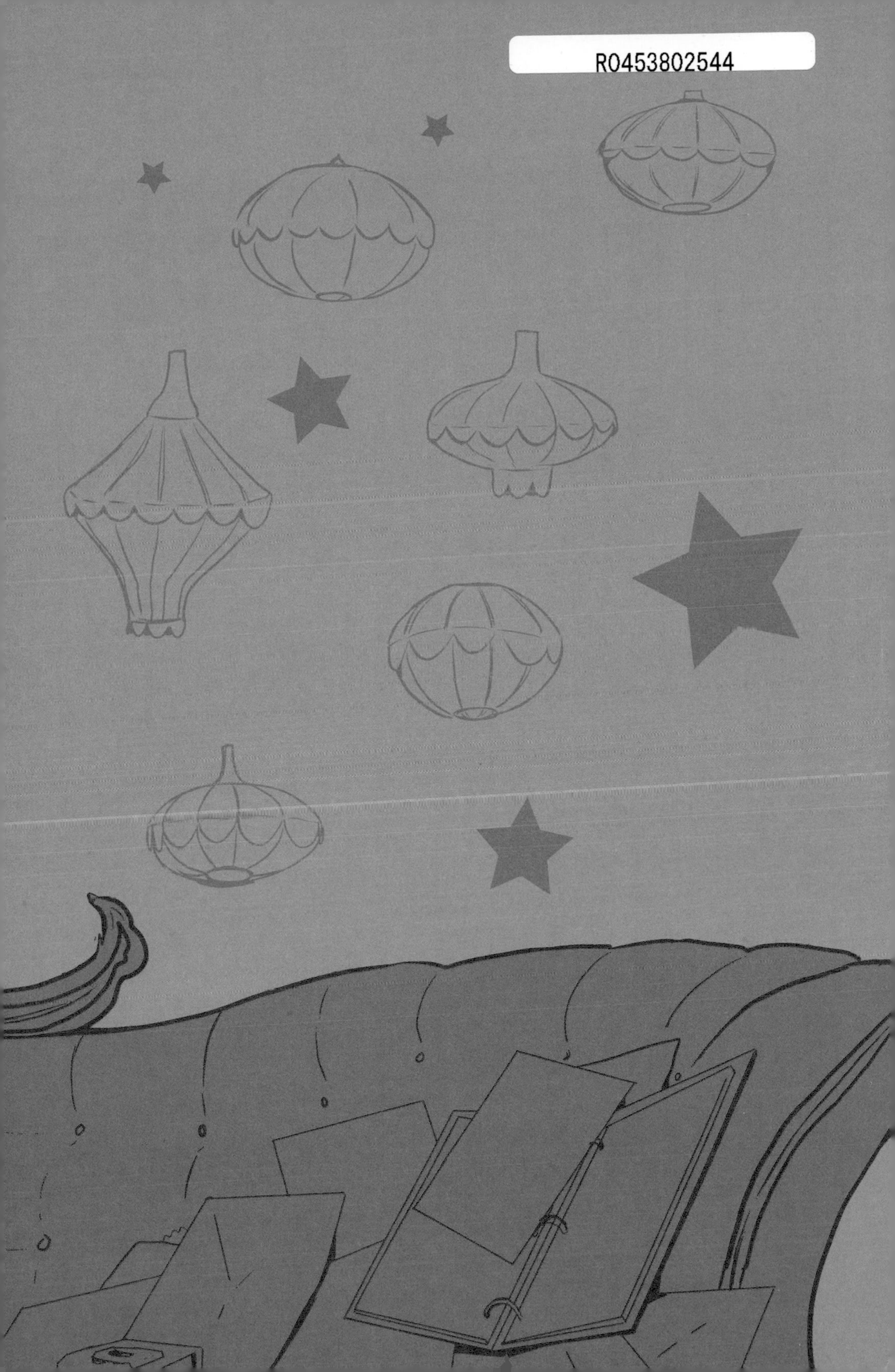

WRITTEN BY
AMBER BENSON & SARAH KUHN

BASED ON THE CHARACTERS
CREATED BY AMY HECKERLING

ILLUSTRATED BY
SIOBHAN KEENAN

COLORED BY
CATHY LE

LETTERED BY
JIM CAMPBELL

COVER BY
NATACHA BUSTOS

DESIGNER
KARA LEOPARD

ASSISTANT EDITOR
SOPHIE PHILIPS-ROBERTS

EDITOR
SHANNON WATTERS

SPECIAL THANKS TO JULIA CHO

INTRODUCTION
BY NICOLE BILDERBACK
"Summer"

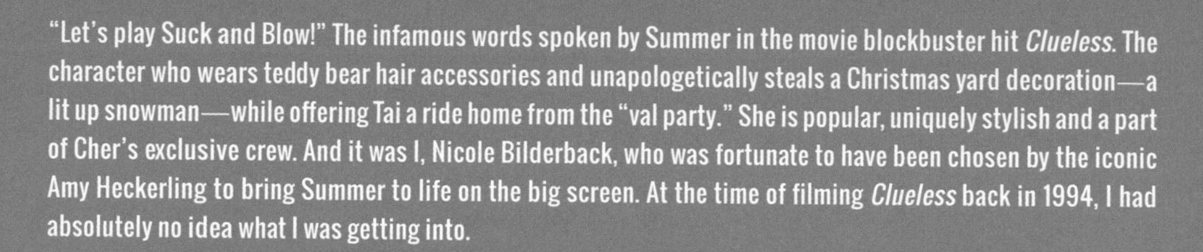

"Let's play Suck and Blow!" The infamous words spoken by Summer in the movie blockbuster hit *Clueless*. The character who wears teddy bear hair accessories and unapologetically steals a Christmas yard decoration—a lit up snowman—while offering Tai a ride home from the "val party." She is popular, uniquely stylish and a part of Cher's exclusive crew. And it was I, Nicole Bilderback, who was fortunate to have been chosen by the iconic Amy Heckerling to bring Summer to life on the big screen. At the time of filming *Clueless* back in 1994, I had absolutely no idea what I was getting into.

I remember my first audition for *Clueless*. I was barely out of high school, having moved to Los Angeles from my hometown of Dallas, Texas. I had only lived in L.A. for a little over a year. I had been building my resume at this point, doing commercials and guest star roles on TV shows. But mainly, I was just happy to be living my dream in Hollywood. I got a call from my agent at the time with an audition appointment for some movie called *Clueless* that Paramount was doing. I just remember thinking, "Oh, it's Paramount Studios, it must be a big production." I was given sides to learn for two different characters, Amber and Summer. I learned lines for both and showed up to the audition with casting director, Marcia Ross. After 24 years, my memories of that day in 1994 are a little hazy, but I remember that Marcia Ross was so lovely, and my read for both roles went great. If memory serves me correctly, she gave me a callback almost immediately, that same day. I don't remember how many days passed between my first audition and the callback. But I remember being asked to prepare lines for a third character named Heather. I would be reading for Amber, Summer, and Heather during my callback with the producers and director.

So, there I was pulling into the Paramount Studios lot for a callback for a movie called *Clueless*, starring the actress from the movie *The Crush*. I would soon learn her name and come to adore Alicia Silverstone. The only thing I remember about the callback was this...Marcia Ross escorted me into the room where I was introduced to the producers and director. I'd heard of Amy Heckerling, the iconic director of *Fast Times at Ridgemont High*, but I was absolutely clueless (pun intended) that I was in the same room with executive producer Scott Rudin (who I would soon discover was one of the biggest producers in the entertainment industry), and associate producer Adam Schroeder (who I would later become friends with). And me. There I was, barely 19 years old, having no clue that I was standing in front of filmmaking legends. All their eyes were on little ol' me. A petite Asian American actress with a Dutch last name who hails from Texas, reading for a supporting role in a Paramount movie with the hopes I would get one of the three characters I was auditioning. One thing I clearly remember about this day was Amy Heckerling microscopically observing me with a big smile on her face.

I was told I was being considered for the role of Amber (my first choice merely because it was a slightly bigger role), along with another actress who was on a soap opera at the time in NYC. She was first choice for Amber, but it was unsure if she was going to be able to commit to the *Clueless* shooting schedule. If she was unavailable to play Amber, then the role was mine. And if she was available, then I would be cast as Summer. To be honest, I didn't really care which role I would play. I liked both. All I knew was that I was being cast as a supporting character in a Paramount movie directed by the legendary Amy Heckerling. I was a happy camper. We all know how it turned out. My very first feature film was *Clueless*. Summer was born. I could not be more happily impacted by all the recognition and support from the fans I still receive to this day. Cheers to this beautiful, funny, witty, gem of a comedy and timeless classic we all know as *Clueless.* The movie that leveled up my career and changed my life.

I would like to give a special thank you to casting director Marcia Ross and producer Adam Schroeder. And of course, to the fiercely talented Amy Heckerling. Thank you for creating Summer and seeing beyond the box that a petite, Asian American actress from Texas could bring her to life on the big screen. I am humbly honored to have been asked to write this introduction by the profoundly talented writers of the *Clueless* comic book series. My deepest gratitude to Sarah Kuhn for reaching out to me, and for giving Summer a newly explored life, allowing the audience and fans to get to know the world of Summer. To my long-time friend Amber Benson, whom I first met on the set of *Buffy The Vampire Slayer* many moons ago, and would later spend many days and nights over the years hanging out with...I am so incredibly proud of you! You've always been one of the most smart, innovative, interesting talents I know. Thank you both for this opportunity of sharing Summer with the world in a new way. With all my heart, I am forever honored.

I present to you, the secret world of Summer.

PROLOGUE

BESTIES 4EVA/LAST SUMMER TOGETHER MIX!
For D & T! <3 C
SONG ONE/SIDE ONE: MONTELL JORDAN-- THIS IS HOW WE DO IT
THIS MIGHT LOOK LIKE A TYPICAL GRADUATION SLUMBER PARTY...**BUT IT WASN'T.**
DUN DUN **DUUUUUUNNNNN!**
I MEAN...IT **WAS** A GRADUATION SLUMBER PARTY. DUH. LIKE, IT WAS TOTALLY THE EVE OF GRADUATION AND THE EX-SENIOR CLASS OF BRONSON ALCOTT HIGH WAS TOTALLY HAVING A SERIOUSLY MAJOR HANG AT CHEZ CHER HOROWITZ. BUT IT WAS ALSO SOMETHING **MORE.**
--AND NAME TWO
THAT WE, LIKE, **PERSONALLY** KNOW...? 'CAUSE NOW THAT WE'VE GRADUATED, I AM SO OVER THE **BOYS** FROM HIGH SCHOOL.
MY DAD'S LAW FIRM REPRESENTS LUKE PERRY **AND** WILL SMITH...SO THAT'S ALMOST EXACTLY LIKE WE GREW UP WITH THEM! TOTALLY COUNTS.
MASH
IT WAS THE BEGINNING OF WHAT WOULD PROVE TO BE A SUMMER OF SPINE-TINGLING MYSTERY, SWOONY ROMANCE, AND GRAND ADVENTURE FOR ME AND MY BF JOSH (AND D AND TAI AND OUR FRIEND SUMMER, TOO)!
OKAY, MAYBE NOW IS A BETTER TIME FOR ME TO SAY... DUN DUN **DUUUUUUNNNNN!**

...um, you guys...
NOT TO BAG ON WHAT WOULD BE AN EXCELLENT ALTERNATE UNIVERSE EXISTENCE, CHER, BUT IN THIS LIFE, YOU DID NOT GROW UP WITH WILL SMITH--
--I BELIEVE IN THE POWER OF POSITIVE THINKING--
--YOU CAN'T THINK YOUR WAY INTO BEING BFFS WITH ALTERNATE UNIVERSE WILL SMITH--
...guys...
YOU GUYS! I AM GONNA MISS YOU SO MUCH!

I DON'T KNOW WHAT I'LL DO. NOT SEEING YOU GUYS **EVERY SINGLE DAY** SOUNDS LIKE THE WORST PUNISHMENT EVER INVENTED.

YOU'RE MY **BEST FRIENDS!**

TAI... AIR...PLEASE... BREATHING... IM...POSSIBLE...

SORRY ABOUT THAT. SOMETIMES I JUST GET REALLY OVER-EMOTIONAL ABOUT THE THREE OF US GOING AWAY TO COMPLETELY DIFFERENT SCHOOLS IN THE FALL. YOU GUYS WILL BE **SO FAR AWAY.**
I THINK MY ENTIRE SHOPPING-PAST JUST FLASHED BEFORE MY EYES.

I FEEL THE SAME WAY, TAI. I'M GONNA MISS YOU BOTH **SO MUCH.** BUT THAT'S WHY WE HAVE A SYNCHRONIZED CALLING SCHEDULE THAT WILL ALLOW US TO SPEAK **AT LEAST** THREE TIMES A DAY...

--AFTER MY MORNING WORKOUT, AT LUNCH/SHOPPING EXCURSIONS BETWEEN CLASSES, RIGHT BEFORE I SLIP MY SLEEP MASK ON FOR BED--
--AND ANYTIME WE JUST FEEL LIKE HEARING EACH OTHER'S VOICES! AND WE'LL WRITE LONG, LONG LETTERS TO EACH OTHER, TOO! WE'LL COME UP WITH SILLY PET NAMES...LIKE **CHER-RY POP** AND **DI-ONIC SQUARED.**
UM.
I WOULDN'T GO **THAT** FAR.
LOOK, NO MATTER WHAT HAPPENS IN THE FALL... THIS SUMMER IS GONNA BE **THE BOMB!**
I HAVE **MY DREAM SUMMER INTERNSHIP** LINED UP WITH ANNE JENNINGS, LEGENDARY BEVERLY HILLS ADVICE COLUMNIST TO THE STARS, AND I'LL BE SPENDING EVERY OTHER SECOND CHILLIN' WITH MY BESTIES!

AND I AM STOKED TO BE PLANNING MY FAMILY'S ANNUAL **END OF SUMMER BEACH BASH.**
THIS IS THE FIRST TIME MY MOTHER HAS ENTRUSTED ME WITH SUCH AN IMPORTANT TASK. BUT THE REST OF MY TIME BELONGS TO MY GIRL GANG.
WITH YOUR MAD LEADERSHIP SKILLS AND PRESIDENTIAL EXPERIENCE, PLANNING THAT PARTY WILL BE CAKE, D.

YOU NEVER KNOW WHAT UNFORESEEN PROBLEMS WILL CROP UP. CONCENTRATION IS **KEY.** THAT AND FOCUS. AND A PRETERNATURAL NOSE FOR DISASTER.
OH, AND MY METICULOUSLY CROSS-INDEXED BINDER OF PLANNING CHARTS, GRAPHS, AND SPREAD-SHEETS.
OKAY, SO A LOT OF THINGS ARE **KEY.** MAYBE **THAT'S** THE KEY?
UGH, NOW I'M CONFUSED.

OF COURSE, YOU NEVER KNOW WHO'S LISTENING OR WHAT HORRORS LIE IN THE HEARTS OF MEN...ER, WOMEN. ER, SUMMER. THAT'S SUMMER AS IN THE PERSON, NOT THE SEASON. EXCEPT WE'RE ALSO TALKING ABOUT THE SEASON, STILL.
FUDGE. D ISN'T THE ONLY ONE WHO'S TOTES CONFUSING HERSELF!
BESIDES SPENDING TIME WITH YOU TWO, I THINK I'M GONNA WORK ON PERFECTING MY BACK NOSEBLUNT SLIDE WITH TRAVIS--
I HOPE THAT'S A SKATEBOARDING TRICK AND NOT SOMETHING SUPER GROSS.
SKATEBOARDING, FOR SURE! BUT WHEN EDWINA GETS TO BH FOR HER FIRST EVER VISIT, I'M GONNA TURN INTO TOUR GUIDE EXTRAORDINAIRE.
I'M SO EXCITED TO SEE EDWINA AGAIN. SHE'S BY FAR MY FAVE OLDER FARMER BABE!
EDWINA IS THE ONLY OLDER FARMER BABE THAT YOU KNOW, CHER.
TRUE, D. BUT IF I DID KNOW OTHER OLDER FARMER BABES, EDWINA WOULD STILL BE MY FAVE!
MY dEAREST SUMMER:
THERE ARE N
EXISTING WO
in THE ENGLISH
LANGUAGE THAT
CAN EXPRESS THE
bEAUTI

HEY GUYS, I DON'T MEAN TO INTERRUPT...
SUMMER! HAPPY GRADUATION AND I LOVE YOUR TOENAILS.

IS THAT HARD CANDY'S CRIMSON LOLLIPOP?

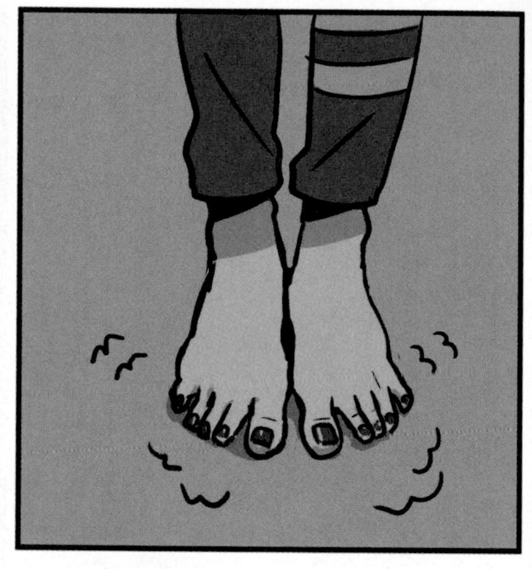

YOU ARE TRULY A MASTER OF THE POLISH.

WE ALL HAVE OUR NOT-SO-HIDDEN TALENTS.
CHER, I WAS WONDERING IF I COULD SPEAK TO YOU IN PRIVATE? IT'S KINDA IMPORTANT.

OF COURSE! AT CHEZ CHER HOROWITZ, YOUR HOSTESS IS ALWAYS HERE TO SERVE!
I WONDER WHAT'S SO HELLA IMPORTANT?
CAN YOU HEAR WHAT THEY'RE SAYING?
EAVESDROPPING IS TRÈS UNCOOL, TAI.
BUT YOU'RE TOTALLY DOING IT TOO, RIGHT?
DUH. OF COURSE.
SO WHAT'S GOING ON IN THE SECRET WORLD OF SUMMER?
I NEED YOUR HELP.

YOU **HAVE** TO READ THIS FIRST TO UNDERSTAND.

MY dEARESt
SUMMER:
ThERE ARE NO
EXiStinG WoRds
in thE EnGLiSH
LAnGUAGE thAT
CAN EXPRESS thE
bEAUtiFoUs
bEAUtY oF yoUR
sMiLE...

A SECRET ADMIRER...?! YOU ARE SO LUCKY!

I WISH I HAD A SECRET ADMIRER!
DON'T YOU HAVE A BOYFRIEND?
WELL... YEAH. BUT EVERYBODY LIKES TO BE ADMIRED!
I DON'T. AT LEAST...NOT THIS TIME.
I SO DON'T UNDERSTAND.
THIS IS THE THIRD LETTER I'VE GOTTEN AND I STILL HAVE NO IDEA WHO SENT THEM! WHAT IF MY SECRET ADMIRER IS MY TRUE LOVE...BUT I NEVER FIGURE OUT WHO THEY ARE?

AND YOU CAME TO ME FOR HELP...BECAUSE OF MY STELLAR MATCH-MAKING SKILLS?
NO, I CAME TO YOU 'CAUSE YOUR DAD IS A BADASS LITIGATOR AND HE PROBABLY KNOWS A TON OF TOP DETECTIVES WHO CAN TAKE ON MY CASE.
I HAVE AN EVEN BETTER IDEA... I AM EXCELLENT AT LOVE AND I WAS ALWAYS A BIG FAN OF NANCY DREW'S BOOKS!

I WILL DISCOVER THE IDENTITY OF YOUR SECRET ADMIRER, SUMMER, OR FOREVER HOLD MY PEACE! GUMSHOE CHER HOROWITZ IS ON THE CASE!
AND WITH THAT, THE GAME WAS AFOOT! UM, I'M PRETTY SURE THAT PARTICULAR SAYING HAS SOMETHING TO DO WITH BEING A GUMSHOE--BUT TO BE HONEST I'M NOT REALLY SEEING HOW PUTTING GUM ON MY LOUBOUTINS HELPS WITH CRIME-SOLVING!

CHAPTER ONE

Your Problem is
My Business
Anne Jennings,
Advice Columnist to the Stars.
How To Become A Good Advice Columnist?
Question #1:
Where does one score the best
advice-giving wardrobe?
June
Cher Horowitz
and the
Mystery of
The Phony Agony Aunt

BESTIES 4EVA/LAST SUMMER TOGETHER MIX!
For D & T! <3 C
SONG TWO/SIDE ONE: NO DOUBT--JUST A GIRL
I KNOW. WE REALLY HAVE TO SPEND AS MUCH TIME HANGING AS POSSIBLE...IT'S *IMPERATIVE.*

IT'S NOT JUST LIKE BEING AT DIFFERENT SCHOOLS...
...IT'S LIKE BEING IN DIFFERENT UNIVERSES!
BEEP
BEEP
BEEP

HOLD UP, D. CALL WAITING.

HELLO?
I WAS JUST SITTING HERE MISSING YOU GUYS ALREADY.
I'M GONNA THREE-WAY YOU WITH ME AND D, TAI. HOLD ON.

TAI, YOU'RE ON WITH ME AND D. I THINK WE ALL FEEL REALLY *LOST...*
--HEY, JOSH, MAKE A RIGHT AT THE NEXT STREET PLEASE--

...BECAUSE WE FEEL LIKE COLLEGE IS *TEARING US APART!*
UM, CHER?

GUYS. JOSH NEEDS A WORD. I'LL CALL YOU BACK.
YES, JOSH?
I DON'T MEAN TO DETRACT FROM THE OBVIOUSLY DIFFICULT SITUATION YOU, D, AND TAI FIND YOURSELVES IN, GOING TO DIFFERENT COLLEGES AND ALL...
BUT AREN'T YOU JUST GOING TO DIFFERENT COLLEGES...IN L.A.?
The Valley
Westwood
Downtown
JOSH, I DON'T THINK YOU UNDERSTAND. DIONNE WILL BE IN WESTWOOD. TAI WILL BE IN THE VALLEY. I WILL BE DOWNTOWN. WE MIGHT AS WELL BE IN DIFFERENT...
...UNIVERSES.
OF COURSE. GOT IT.

STOP!
THAT'S ANNE JENNINGS' HOUSE!
HOLY--
YOU JUST SCARED THE HELL OUTTA ME, CHER.
SCREECH
SORRY, JOSH! I'M LATE!

I WANT YOU TO KNOW THAT I TRULY APPRECIATE YOU BEING MY CHAUFFEUR THIS SUMMER.

DADDY IS BEING A REAL PAIN ABOUT WHAT WAS JUST--

--A TEENSY WEENSY LITTLE FENDER BENDER.
EXACTLY!

OKAY, I GOTTA RUN, TOO. I'M SUPPOSED TO BE AT YOUR DAD'S OFFICE...OH, SOMETHING LIKE TWENTY MINUTES AGO.

SEE YOU AT FIVE! LOVE YOU!
LOVE YOU, TOO...
...YOU BANANAS WOMAN, YOU.

NOK
NOK
NOK

creee-eak
?

OH, THANK GOD YOU'RE HERE.
MS. JENNINGS?
HI, MY NAME IS CHER--

--HOROWITZ AND--

--UH--

I'D NEVER MADE COFFEE BEFORE WITHOUT LUCY'S HELP. BUT I WAS A HIGH SCHOOL GRADUATE NOW. A TOTALLY SELF-SUFFICIENT ADULT-TYPE PERSON. WHAT COULD GO WRONG?

PTOOEY!
OKAY, SO MAYBE MAKING COFFEE WAS HARDER THAN IT LOOKED.

COFFEE! **I NEED COFFEE!** GO NOW--THE KITCHEN--PLEASE! BEFORE I FAINT **DEAD AWAY** FROM LACK OF CAFFEINE!
MEDIUM HALF-CAFF SOY LATTE AT 120 DEGREES, MAGGIE NEEDS A WALK--AND DON'T FORGET MY DRY CLEANING. **HURRY, HURRY, HURRY...** I CAN HARDLY STAND. MY BRAIN IS A FOG. I AM ON THE **VERY PRECIPICE** OF DEATH!
I'D ALWAYS FELT LIKE MY DESTINY WAS IN THE WORLD OF HIGH-END ADVICE GIVING...

...AND OBVS--WITH THIS INTERNSHIP--I WAS SUPPOSED TO BE LEARNING FROM ONE OF THE MOST RESPECTED MASTERS ABOUT HOW TO HELP PEOPLE...
...HOW TO DISPENSE ADVICE THAT CHANGED LIVES...

MAGGIE-- WAIT FOR ME!
...WHILE ALSO LEARNING HOW TO GET SWEET INVITES TO ALL THE BEST HOLLYWOOD BASHES AND ASSEMBLE MY MOST COLUMNIST-WORTHY WARDROBE.
BUT THIS GLORIFIED ERRAND GIRL ROUTINE WAS SO NOT ME!

HELLO...? MS. JENNINGS? I HAVE YOUR MEDIUM HALF-CAFF SOY LATTE AND YOUR--
--DRY CLEANING--
--AND--

--NO, MAGGIE, NO!

WHOOOSH

WHERE DID YOU GO TO GET THAT COFFEE? NEW ZEALAND?
IF THAT DRINK IS COLD, I'M DOCKING YOUR PAY, CLARE!

CLARE?! DID SHE JUST CALL ME 'CLARE'? OH, THIS WOULD TOTES NOT DO AT ALL! ANNE JENNINGS, ADVICE COLUMNIST TO THE STARS, YOU NEED TO TAKE A BIG OLD GIANT--

--CHILL PILL! ARGH! I'M SUPPOSED TO BE LEARNING VALUABLE LIFE LESSONS, HERE! SHE DIDN'T WORK ON HER COLUMN ONCE TODAY. JUST KEPT ORDERING ME AROUND AND STARING AT HER MAGIC 8-BALL!
NO ONE IS PERFECT, CHER. MAYBE THAT'S PART OF HER PROCESS...? AND ANYWAY, I DOUBT SHE CALLED YOU CLARE ON PURPOSE--

OR IF SHE DID, MAYBE IT WAS ONLY A JOKE...?

CHER, I'VE HAD BAD BOSSES...PEOPLE WHO MADE ME FEEL TWO INCHES TALL AND YELLED AT ME CONSTANTLY. IT SUCKS, BUT SOMETIMES YOU JUST HAVE TO GRIN AND BEAR IT UNTIL IT'S OVER. SOMETIMES THAT'S THE LIFE LESSON.

JUST BE GLAD IT'S ONLY FOR THE SUMMER. GRINNING FOR LONGER THAN THAT CAN REALLY MAKE YOUR FACE HURT.
YOU'RE SO RIGHT, JOSH. CHER HOROWITZ DOES NOT ACCEPT DEFEAT SO EASILY! I'LL JUST FLIP THE SWITCH ON THIS NIGHTMARE!
BE HELLA NICE TO ANNE JENNINGS AND SHOW HER THAT A WORKPLACE IS WAY SWEETER WHEN EVERYONE GETS ALONG.
OH, WELL, YEAH, I MEAN, IF THAT'S WHAT I SAID, THEN... YEAH, GO FOR IT.
RRRING RING RING

CHER HOROWITZ-- INTERN TO ANNE JENNINGS, ADVICE COLUMNIST TO THE STARS-- SPEAKING...?
UM, YES, THIS IS CLARE, MS. JENNINGS.
AND THE ATROCITIES DIDN'T STOP THERE. DAY ONE WAS EXTREME...
BESTIES 4EVA/LAST SUMMER TOGETHER MIX!
For D & T! <3 C
SONG THREE/SIDE ONE: THE CRANBERRIES--ZOMBIE

...BUT BY THE END OF MY FIRST WEEK, THE SITUATION WAS **HEINOUS.**
RRRING RING RING
BEEP BEEP BEEP
ZZZZZZZZZ ZZZZ-ZZZ ZZZ...

ZZZZZZZZZ ZZZZ-ZZZZZZ ZZZZZ-ZZZZZZ ZZZZZZZZZ...
IT DIDN'T MATTER WHAT TIME OF DAY OR NIGHT. AS FAR AS ANNE JENNINGS, ADVICE COLUMNIST TO THE STARS, WAS CONCERNED, I WAS AT HER BECK AND CALL 24/7.

The Record
AND FORGET MY GRAND PLAN TO BE HELLA NICE TO HER. THERE WAS **NO TIME** TO BE NICE TO HER. BECAUSE I WAS TOO BUSY GETTING HER COFFEE. AND HER DRY CLEANING. AND HER PUPPY'S EXTREMELY HARD-TO-FIND FAVORITE SPECIALTY KIBBLE. AND--

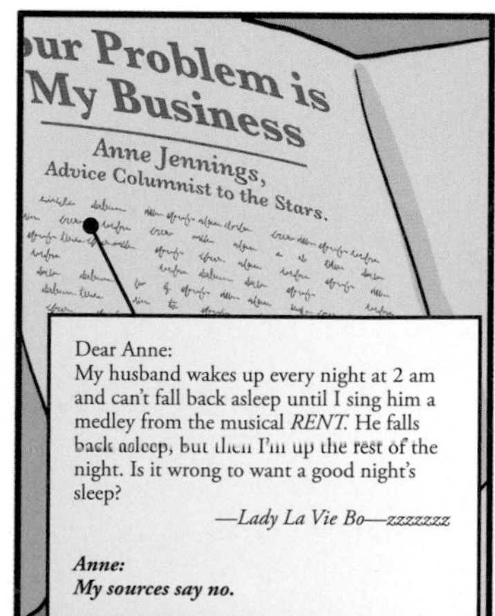
our Problem is My Business
Anne Jennings, Advice Columnist to the Stars.
Dear Anne:
My husband wakes up every night at 2 am and can't fall back asleep until I sing him a medley from the musical *RENT.* He falls back asleep, but then I'm up the rest of the night. Is it wrong to want a good night's sleep?
—*Lady La Vie Bo—zzzzzzz*
Anne:
My sources say no.
THAT ANSWER WAS...STRANGELY FAMILIAR. AS SHAKESPEARE SO WISELY SAID: SOMETHING SMELLED FUNNY IN THE STATE OF BEVERLY HILLS...

SO I DID WHAT I ALWAYS DO WHEN THINGS GET SUPER GNARLY... I ASSEMBLED MY GIRL GANG! OH, AND JOSH.
Your Problem is My Business
Anne Jennings, Advice Columnist to the Stars.
GANG, I HAVE ASSEMBLED YOU HERE BECAUSE I HAVE A MAJOR PROBLEM... I THINK ANNE JENNINGS, ADVICE COLUMNIST TO THE STARS, MIGHT NOT BE DISPENSING HER OWN ADVICE.
Your Problem My Business
Anne Jennings, Advice Columnist to the Stars.
EVIDENCE #1: ANNE'S LATEST ADVICE COLUMN. POOR LA VIE BO--ZZZZZZZ NEEDED REAL HELP. SHE WAS EXHAUSTED FROM SINGING LIGHT MY CANDLE, AND I BELIEVE THAT INSTEAD OF DIGGING DEEP AND FINDING THE RIGHT WORDS OF WISDOM, ANNE TURNED TO--

--EVIDENCE #2: THIS MAGIC 8-BALL. WHERE SHE GOT AN ANSWER THAT WAS NOT AT ALL HELPFUL TO LA VIE BO--ZZZZZZZ.

MY SOURCES SAY NO.

YES, TAI?
I DIG THE MAGNIFYING GLASS. *TRÈS* MYSTERY-SOLVING CHIC.

IF I WANT TO THINK LIKE A DETECTIVE, THEN I MUST BECOME ONE WITH A DETECTIVE. SO I AM CHANNELING ONE OF THE MOST FAMOUS DETECTIVES IN HISTORY: **NANCY DREW!**

YOU KNOW SHE'S NOT A REAL PERSON, RIGHT?
UH, YES, OF COURSE I KNEW ***THAT.*** I MEANT: ONE OF THE MOST FAMOUS DETECTIVES IN ***LITERARY*** HISTORY.
AND...WHAT'S TO DETECT? IF YOU ALREADY KNOW WHAT'S GOING ON?
I ONLY HAVE A HUNCH. **WE NEED PROOF!**

ARE YOU GUYS SURE YOU WANT TO PLAY DETECTIVE? WHAT IF YOU GET IN TROUBLE? WHY NOT JUST LEAVE THIS LADY ALONE WITH HER BAD ADVICE AND--
JOSH! HOW COULD YOU?! THINK OF ALL THE BAD ADVICE RECEIVERS OUT THERE! IT'S OUR DUTY TO HELP THEM!

IF MY GIRL CHER IS WORRIED THAT SOMEONE IS MENACING THE GOOD PEOPLE OF BEVERLY HILLS WITH BAD ADVICE, THEN WE MUST **STOP THEM!** MURRAY AND I ARE IN.
ME AND TRAVIS, TOO!

BESTIES 4EVA/LAST SUMMER TOGETHER MIX!
For D & T! <3 C
SONG FOUR/SIDE ONE: DURAN DURAN--WATCHING THE DETECTIVES
MY BESTIES D AND TAI WERE ON THE CASE...BUT SOMETHING ABOUT JOSH'S RETICENCE WAS WAY HARSHING MY MELLOW. WHICH MADE ME WONDER: WHAT WAS JOSH HIDING THAT HE DIDN'T WANT DETECTIVE CHER TO DISCOVER?!?
"WHEN DINING WITH BRITISH ROYALTY...DO NOT EAT ASPARAGUS WITH A UTENSIL. DO USE YOUR FINGERS."
Dear Anne:
I have a crush on my co-worker, but he doesn't seem to know I exist. Any advice to catch his eye?
—Cubically Challenged in Love
Anne:
Use your fingers.

I AM USING THIS NEWSPAPER AS A DISTRACTIONARY DEVICE, MURRAY. IT'S IMPERATIVE THAT I MAINTAIN MY COVER.
BUT I JUST WANNA LOOK AT THE SPORTS SECTION, BABY. FOR FIVE SECONDS. C'MON!
--AND, I TELL YOU, THAT CROOKED SENATOR IS GONNA END UP ON THE WRONG SIDE OF A CRIMINAL CASE ONE DAY.
THEY'RE GONNA THROW THE BOOK AT 'EM. SENTENCE 'EM TO THE FULLEST EXTENT OF THE LAW.
Dear Anne:
My daughter received twenty dollars too much in change at the grocery store. Is it wrong to keep the money?
—It's Only A Twenty
Anne:
Your daughter is going to end up on the wrong side of a criminal case. They are going to throw the book at her and then sentence her to the fullest extent of the law.

BUT, DARLING, ASTA THINKS WE--
HEY, JOSH?

click

WHAT ARE YOU WATCHING?
NOTHING. I WAS WATCHING NOTHING--
--BUT I CLEARLY HEARD THE TELEVISION ON AND YOU ARE HOLDING THE REMOTE CONTROL IN YOUR HAND--
--SO WHAT DID YOU WANT TO ASK ME?

NOTHING. I WANTED TO TELL YOU THAT IT'S TIME FOR US TO TAKE OVER THE STAKEOUT FROM D AND MURRAY.
OH, UH, RIGHT. GIVE ME A COUPLE TO GET READY.

JOSH WAS FOR SURE ACTING SQUIRRELLY. BUT I WAS CHANNELING MY GIRL DETECTIVE MOJO, SO I KNEW IT WAS JUST A MATTER OF TIME BEFORE I GOT TO THE BOTTOM OF BOTH MYSTERIES. MAYBE DETECTING WAS MY REAL CAREER CALLING!
I WISH YOU'D TELL ME WHAT SHOW YOU WERE WATCHING--
I TOLD YOU. IT WAS NOTHING--
IT OBVIOUSLY WASN'T NOTHING--
BEEPBEEPBEEPBEEPBEEP
WHAT THE HECK IS THAT?!
MY BEEPER!
SWIII-OOOSH
SUMMER 9-11
WHO'S OUT THERE?!
CLARE HOROWAY, I DON'T KNOW WHAT YOU THINK YOU'RE DOING OUT HERE IN THE DEAD OF NIGHT, BUT YOU ARE FIRED!

I'D GOTTEN SO CAUGHT UP IN 'DETECTING' THAT I'D TOTALLY BLOWN OUR COVER.
PLUS, I'D COMPLETELY FORGOTTEN ABOUT MY PROMISE TO HELP SUMMER DISCOVER THE IDENTITY OF HER SECRET ADMIRER.
AND THAT'S WHEN I REALIZED I DIDN'T HAVE A CLUE HOW TO BE A GOOD DETECTIVE...OR A GOOD FRIEND!
I HAD TOTES HARSHED MY OWN GIG!
DUN DUN... DUN?
BESTIES 4EVA/LAST SUMMER TOGETHER MIX!
For D & T! <3
SONG FIVE/SIDE ONE: BECK--LOSER

CHAPTER TWO

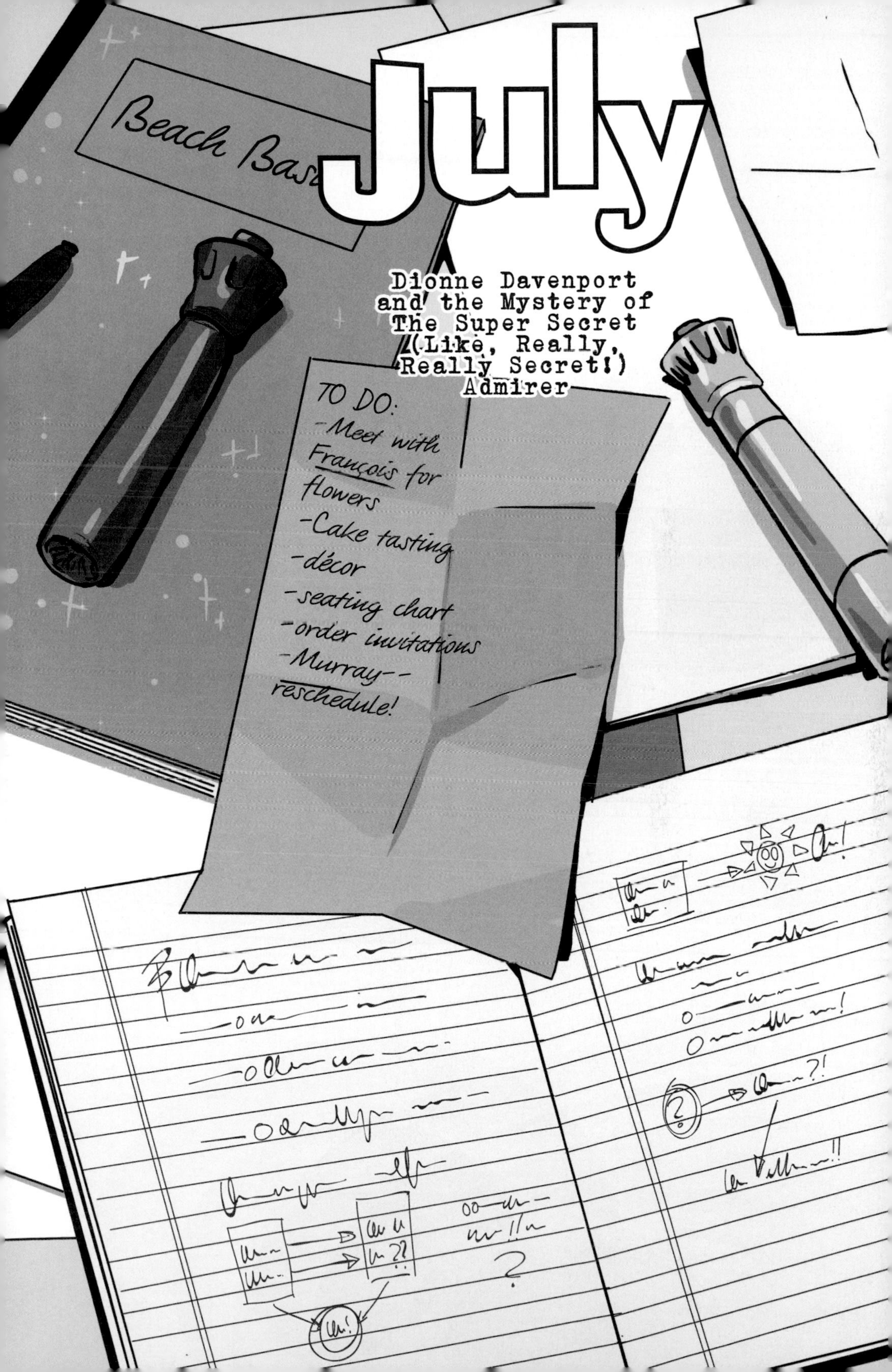
Beach Bash
July
Dionne Davenport and the Mystery of The Super Secret (Like, Really, Really Secret!) Admirer
TO DO:
-Meet with François for flowers
-Cake tasting
-décor
-seating chart
-order invitations
-Murray--reschedule!

IT IS A TRUTH UNIVERSALLY ACKNOWLEDGED, THAT A YOUNG WOMAN ON THE CUSP OF COLLEGEDOM, MUST BE IN WANT OF EXTRA HOURS IN THE DAY IN ORDER TO ACCOMPLISH ABSOLUTELY EVERYTHING ON HER TERRIFYINGLY EXTENSIVE TO-DO LIST.
OKAY, OKAY--SO MAYBE THAT'S NOT THE MOST UNIVERSAL OF TRUTH BOMBS. BUT IT'S **MY** TRUTH. LET'S ROLL WITH IT.
CHECK IT, BABY! LOCATING WINTER WEAR IN L.A.--PARTICULARLY IN THE MIDDLE OF THE HOTTEST OF SUMMER CLIMES--IS A FEAT OF NEAR IMPOSSIBILITY, BUT WE ACED IT!
DO I LOOK LIKE **FULL-ON ROYALTY** OR WHAT?
SONG ONE/SIDE ONE: RuPAUL--SUPERMODEL (YOU BETTER WORK)

WHY DO YOU NEED A WINTER COAT?
BEEP BEEP BEEP
FOR NOVA SCOTIA! WHERE I'M HEADED FOR MY HIGHER EDUCATION! WHICH WE'VE TALKED ABOUT LIKE FIVE MILLION KAZILLION TIMES! OR AT LEAST I'VE TALKED ABOUT IT...

THIS BETTER NOT BE FRANÇOIS ABOUT THE CENTERPIECES AGAIN, OR I SWEAR ON ALL THAT IS HOLY, BUT MOST ESPECIALLY MY VINTAGE CHANEL, I AM GOING TO KILL--
--OH. CHER SOS.

OKAY. OKAY. I CAN SCHEDULE IN EXACTLY FORTY-FIVE MINUTES FOR A CHER SOS-RELATED CRISIS TODAY--ADD IT TO MY TO-DO LIST. I JUST HAVE TO MOVE MY TRIP TO PARTY PARTY WAREHOUSE TO THE AFTERNOON...
I THOUGHT WE WERE GOING TO COMMUNE TOGETHER NUTRITIONALLY--Y'KNOW, GET LUNCH AND TALK? ABOUT HOW WE'RE GOING TO MANAGE OUR LONG-DISTANCE LOVE.

SORRY--GOTTA BOUNCE, BABY. I'VE ENTERED HEAVY BEACH BASH PLANNING MODE AND THAT MEANS EVERY SINGLE SECOND OF MY LIFE IS RULED BY THE TO-DO LIST...
CATCH YA ON THE FLIP!

I DON'T GET IT, CHER, YOU'RE STILL SNOOPING ON ANNE JENNINGS? DIDN'T SHE FIRE YOU?
I'M NOT "FIRED," TAI--WE'RE GOING THROUGH A TEMPORARY TRIAL SEPARATION AS EMPLOYER AND EMPLOYEE--
THAT SOUNDS A LOT LIKE "FIRED"--
AND THIS WHOLE SITUATION HAS MADE IT CLEAR THAT ANNE NEEDS MY HELP AS MUCH AS HER BESIEGED ADVISEES DO! BUT I HAVE TO DEVISE A WAY TO SNOOP--I MEAN INVESTIGATE HER FROM AFAR.
Beach Basics

SO TODAY WE'RE GOING TO TAKE ON CASE NUMERO TWO IN DETECTIVE CHER'S FILES: THE MYSTERY OF SUMMER'S SECRET ADMIRER! JOSH IS GOING TO ACCOMPANY US--
JOSH IS GOING TO DROP YOU OFF, ACTUALLY, I'VE GOT A TON OF WORK TO DO.

MY SKILLS OF DEDUCTION HAVE HELPED ME, ER, DEDUCE THAT SUMMER'S AT THE BEACH TODAY!
OOOH, THE BEACH! SWIMMING AND VOLLEYBALL AND THOSE ADORABLE LITTLE COOKIES SHAPED LIKE SEALS FROM THE SNACK BAR--
TAI, THIS IS AN IMPORTANT INVESTIGATION! WE'RE NOT GOING FOR FUN!
Beach Basics

OH, WELL... AT LEAST YOU'RE PLANNING SOME FUN AT THE BEACH, RIGHT, D? THE SUMMER BEACH BASH?
AFFIRMATIVE. I'M CURRENTLY CROSS-REFERENCING MY LIST OF VENDORS TO ENSURE THAT ALL GOODS AND SERVICES ARE DELIVERED AT THE CORRECT TIME AND THE FUN CAN PROCEED ON SCHEDULE.

AND IT'S GOTTEN TO THE POINT WHERE I GET A LETTER, LIKE, EVERY OTHER DAY--
SUMMER'S FAB HAIR ACCOUTREMENTS!
WOW, SUMMER, NOT TO DERAIL OUR TRAIN OF DAZZLING DETECTION, BUT THESE HAIR ACCESSORIES ARE OFF-THE-CHARTS BODACIOUS--YOU MAKE THEM ALL YOURSELF?!
TOTES! MY ULTIMATE DREAM SCENARIO IS TO BE THE QUEENPIN OF A BALLER FASHION EMPIRE, LIKE MY MOM AND AUNTIE--THEY OWN THAT MAD SUCCESSFUL CHAIN OF BOUTIQUES? BUT THIS SECRET ADMIRER MESS HAS ME TOTALLY BUGGIN'--
BONK
OW!

SUMMER! ARE YOU OKAY?
YEAH, JUST...UH, MY HEAD. NOT LIKE I WAS USING THAT OR ANYTHING.
PER **OFFICIAL LIFEGUARD CODE,** I AM GOING TO VANQUISH THE PERPETRATORS--THAT IS, ISSUE A STERNLY WORDED WARNING--BUT FIRST I WANTED TO MAKE SURE YOU ARE ONE HUNDRED PERCENT UNHURT.
TOTALLY FINE. GO MAKE WITH THE VANQUISHING.

UH, SUMMER...
WHO... **WHO...**
OH, THAT'S JUST BEN.
HELLO, THAT SMOKIN' HOT BALDWIN ISN'T "JUST" ANYTHING...
HE'S AN OLD FAMILY FRIEND. WE'VE KNOWN EACH OTHER SINCE WE WERE FIVE.

MY DETECTIVE SUPER SENSES ARE **TINGLING!** BEN WAS JUST PAYING YOU SOME **EXTREMELY ATTENTIVE ATTENTION,** SUMMER!
COULD HE BE YOUR SECRET ADMIRER?! **OOH!** IT'S FATED, JUST LIKE **ROMEO AND JULIET!**
UM, CHER, DID YOU READ **ROMEO AND JULIET?**
I READ THE BEGINNING! SOOOOO PREDICTABLE. I COULD TOTALLY SEE HOW IT WAS GOING TO END.
IT'S NOT BEN.

"CHILDHOOD! WE PLAYED 'WEDDING' WHEN WE WERE SIX. OUR STUFFED ANIMALS OFFICIATED. THEY BLESSED THE UNION, BUT IT WAS BUSTED BEFORE IT EVEN BEGAN!
I MEAN. BEN AND I HAVE NEVER PROGRESSED BEYOND THE PLANE OF THE PLATONIC. AND WE'VE HAD MAD OPPORTUNITIES.
"THE SUPES AWK PRE-TEEN YEARS! OUR PARENTALS GRANTED US PERMISSION TO ATTEND OUR FIRST R-RATED FLICK--IF WE WENT TOGETHER. ALAS, OUR HANDS BARELY BRUSHED OVER THE POPCORN.
"FROSH YEAR PROM! I THOUGHT HE WANTED TO PLANT ONE ON ME DURING THE SLOWEST OF JAMS--BUT NADA! THEN HIS FAM MOVED AWAY AND I FIGURED THAT WAS THAT.
"AND NOW! HE'S BACK FOR COLLEGE--AND HE'S BOARDING AT MY FAMILIAL ABODE! WE STAY UP LATE TALKING ABOUT EVERYTHING... BUT NO MOVES HAVE BEEN MADE. EVER."
D's Summer Mix
SONG TWO/SIDE ONE: ROXETTE--IT MUST HAVE BEEN LOVE

SO... ROMANTIC...
MY BAD, THAT IS LIKE ROMEO AND JULIET--WITHOUT ALL THE DEATH AND STUFF.
WHAT?!
NOTHING.

IT'S NOT BEN! I KNOW IT'S NOT. I MADE A SEVENTY-TWO PART LIST DETAILING ALL THE REASONS IT'S NOT HIM, COMPLETE WITH PIE CHARTS--
A LIST WITH PIE CHARTS?! GIRL, YOU AND I ARE ON THE SAME LEVEL.
THEN WHO IS IT?

MAYBE ONE OF THESE BEACH RATS WHO'S HERE ALL THE TIME? ELTON AND HIS CREW COULD HAVE GLIMPSED THE GLORY OF YOUR BETTY-NESS FROM AFAR...
THOUGH IF THAT'S THE CASE: I ENCOURAGE YOU TO MAKE LIKE FLO-JO AND RUN AWAY SUPER-FAST! ELTON IS A CREEPOLA OF THE HIGHEST DEGREE!
UGH, NO ENCOURAGEMENT NEEDED. THEY'RE A BUNCH OF BOGUS BARNEYS.
WAIT, WHAT'S THIS...

SUMMER

SUMMER

MY DETECTIVE SUPER SENSES ARE TINGLING! THIS MUST BE A NEW NOTE FROM YOUR SECRET ADMIRER, A CLUE--
POP
IT'S JUST MORE OF THE SAME-- ALL ABOUT MY SMILE! AND MY EYES! AND MY...EVERYTHING! I NEED THIS HALF-BAKED POET TO BECOME, LIKE...FULLY BAKED! AND REVEAL HIMSELF!
WHAT IS THIS MYSTERIOUS SUBSTANCE?! DETECTIVE CHER NEEDS TO FURTHER ANALYZE THE CHEMICAL MAKEUP OF--
IT'S CONFETTI, CHER.
BUT...HMM. IT LOOKS LIKE A MOST DISTINCTIVE TYPE OF CONFETTI.

CHECK IT: I NEED TO BOOK IT TO PARTY PARTY WAREHOUSE TO PICK UP SOME CHOICE DECOR FOR THE BEACH BASH--
EW, D! SHOPPING OFF THE RACK?!
Beach Basics
AS IF! THIS PLACE ONLY STOCKS THE MOST PREMIUM OF PARTY SUPPLIES! BUT WHILE I'M THERE, I'LL SEE IF I CAN FIND A MATCH FOR THIS CONFETTI! PERHAPS THAT WILL LEAD OUR INVESTIGATORY PURSUITS IN A NEW DIRECTION...
BEEP BEEP BEEP

BEEP BEEP BEEP
OOH! YOU ARE SUCH A MASTER OF MULTI-TASKING!
BEEP BEEP
NOT SO MASTERFUL A MASTER-- I TOTES SPACED ON HANG TIME WITH MURRAY LATER! AND HE'S BLOWIN' UP MY BEEPER! I'LL HAVE TO FIGURE SOMETHING OUT...
MEANWHILE, I NEED TO FIGURE OUT WHY JOSH IS ACTING SO WEIRD. AND FIND A MORE CLIMATE-APPROPRIATE DETECTING ENSEMBLE. THESE LAYERS ARE TOE-UP!
UM, WHERE'S TAI?
HEY, GUYS!
DID YOU SOLVE THE MYSTERY YET?

YES, SO I'D JUST ADDED YET ANOTHER ITEM TO MY ALREADY GINORMOUS TO-DO LIST--BUT ALL GOOD LEADERS ARE, AS CHER PUT IT, MASTERS OF MULTITASKING! AND I WOULD BE NO DIFFERENT...
PARTY
UM, BABY? YOU KNOW I'D GO ANYWHERE FOR YOU--EVEN THE DEEP VALLEY. BUT THIS ISN'T EXACTLY WHAT I HAD IN MIND FOR OUR ROMANTIC LUNCH. AND WE STILL NEED TO TALK--
WE CAN TALK WHILE WE'RE GETTING THINGS DONE!

NOW. WE NEED TINY PLASTIC SURFBOARDS, TINY PLASTIC FLAMINGOS, TINY PLASTIC STARFISH, AND MOST IMPORTANTLY--
--A TINY PLASTIC BEACH TO PUT ALL OF IT IN?
NO, DON'T BE SILLY! FRANÇOIS IS BRINGING THE TINY PLASTIC BEACH WITH HIM! IT'S AN INTEGRAL PART OF THE CENTERPIECES.

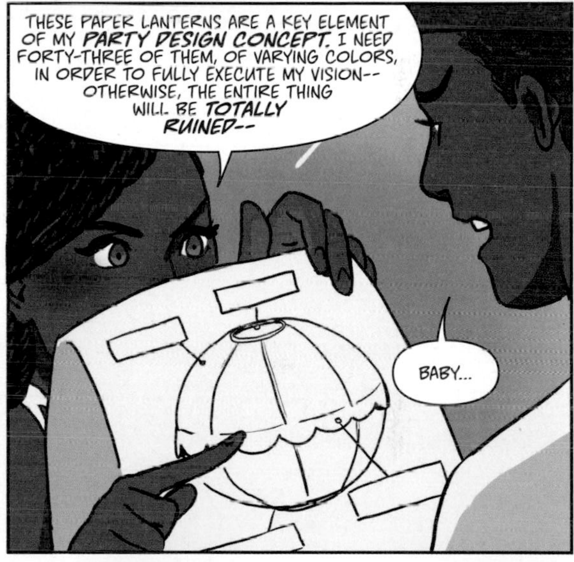
THESE PAPER LANTERNS ARE A KEY ELEMENT OF MY PARTY DESIGN CONCEPT. I NEED FORTY-THREE OF THEM, OF VARYING COLORS, IN ORDER TO FULLY EXECUTE MY VISION--OTHERWISE, THE ENTIRE THING WILL BE TOTALLY RUINED--
BABY...

CHILL. YOU GOT THIS. AND I GOT YOU.

OKAY. LET'S GO!
SO...ABOUT THAT TALK WE NEEDED TO HAVE...

ME BEING WAY UP NORTH AND YOU BEING HERE MEANS WE'LL BE LOCATIONALLY CHALLENGED, BUT--
LAST YEAR'S BEACH BASH HAD THREE HUNDRED FLAMINGOS, LET'S MAKE IT FIVE HUNDRED THIS YEAR!
OOH! FAKE DRIFTWOOD WILL PROVIDE THAT TRUE BIT OF SHABBY CHIC RUSTICAL CHARM! LIKE WE'RE EXPERIENCING NATURE!
WHOA, YOU KNOW WHAT HAS A TON OF NATURE YOU CAN PEEP ON THE REGULAR?! NOVA SCOTIA! WHICH--BABY, BE CAREFUL...
THE GIGANTIC PINEAPPLE DEFINITELY MAKES A HELLA DECLARATIVE STATEMENT, BUT IS THE SMALL PINEAPPLE MORE TASTEFUL? UGH, SUCH A DECORATIVE DILEMMA!
SPEAKING OF DILEMMAS--I MEAN, IT'S NOT A DILEMMA JUST YET, BUT WE REALLY NEED TO CONVERSE ABOUT--
SHHH, MURRAY! I'M TRYING TO LET THE PINEAPPLES SPEAK TO ME...

CHECK... CHECK... CHECK...
BUT WE STILL NEED...

THOSE!

THE PAPER LANTERNS! PERFECTO! AND THEY HAVE PLENTY LEFT...

UH...
SWOOP

HEY! YOU CAN'T BOGART ALL OF THOSE!
SAYS YOU, YOUNG MISSY!

I'M PLANNING A VERY IMPORTANT SHINDIG--
SO ARE WE!

THE ANNUAL DAVENPORT END OF SUMMER BEACH BASH IS THE PARTY OF THE YEAR--
THE GLENDALE SENIOR CENTER KARAOKE JAM-OFF IS THE PARTY OF THE CENTURY--
I'VE NEVER HEARD OF IT!
THEN I'LL SAY IT LOUDER!

SWOOSH
BABY...
SENIOR CENTER CREW, CIRCLE UP! THE YOUTHFUL INTERLOPER IS TRYING TO TAKE OUR LANTERNS!
THEY'RE NOT YOURS!
CRASH

SCREECH

SMACK
CRASH
WHOOM
BABY! DIONNE!
UGH. BESTED BY A POSSE OF BELLIGERENT SENIOR CITIZENS. NOT MY FINEST HOUR.
ALTHOUGH...

I'D FAILED ONE OF MY MAJOR MISSIONS--BUT THANKS TO MY MULTI-TASKING MOJO, I'D MANAGED TO PULL OUT A TRIUMPH ELSEWHERE! I COULD CROSS AT LEAST ONE THING OFF MY TO-DO LIST...BUT I STILL HAD ABOUT A ZILLION TASKS TO GO...
AND SO, ONCE I DETERMINED THAT THE VERY DISTINCTIVE CONFETTI USED BY SUMMER'S ADMIRER IS MOS DEF STOCKED AT PARTY PARTY WAREHOUSE, I PROCURED THE STORE'S RECEIPTS TO SEE IF ANYONE WE'RE ACQUAINTED WITH HAD PURCHASED SAID CONFETTI--
WHOA, D! HOW DID YOU CONVINCE THE MANAGER TO PONY UP TOTALLY CLASSIFIED INTEL?! DETECTIVE CHER IS IN AWE!

MY PRESIDENTIAL PROWESS MEANS I CAN TALK ANYONE INTO ANYTHING!
EXCEPT STRAIGHT-UP BUGGIN' SENIOR CITIZENS, APPARENTLY...

SO, DID YOU SUMMON US TO SUMMER'S PAD BECAUSE YOU WANT US TO HELP YOU COMB THROUGH THE RECEIPTS? ASSESS THE INFO? CLASSIFY THE DATA? ER...SOME OTHER PHRASE THAT SOUNDS IMPORTANT?
CORRECT, TAI, BUT THAT'S NOT ALL WE'RE HERE TO DO!

MY BEACH BASH PLANNING TASKS FOR TODAY INCLUDE CAKE TASTING AND PARTY FAVOR ASSEMBLAGE--SO WE'RE GOING TO DO ALL OF THOSE THINGS AT ONCE!

ER, THREE THINGS AT ONCE? I MEAN, I'VE TOTES HOT GLUE GUNNED A PAIR OF PARTICULARLY GNARLY HAIR ACCESSORIES WHILE SIMULTANEOUSLY MARATHONING CINDY C'S MOST COMPLEX EPS OF HOUSE OF STYLE, BUT--
CHILL, SUMMER. I HAVE A SYSTEM.

LOOK AT RECEIPTS: CHECK! TAKE A BITE OF CAKE: CHECK! THEN SET DOWN YOUR FORK--

--AND ASSEMBLE THE PARTY FAVOR!

AND CHE--
GAAAAAAHHH!
BEEP BEEP BEEP BEEP BEEP BEEP BEEP BEEP

MURRAY! THAT BOY IS TRIPPIN'. I TOLD HIM MY TO-DO LIST WAS GOING TO KEEP ME TIED UP FOR THE REST OF THE DAY!
GO, GO, GO! I HAVE AN HOUR BUDGETED TO COMPLETE ALL OF THESE TASKS! THEN I NEED TO GO MEET WITH FRANÇOIS AND TRY TO FIND ANOTHER REPUTABLE SOURCE FOR PAPER LANTERNS...
D's Summer Mix!
SONG THREE/SIDE ONE: QUEEN LATIFAH--U.N.I.T.Y.

SUMMER-AH! BEN IS HOME!
HE'S HAD SUCH A HARD DAY, SAVING ALL THOSE DROWNING PEOPLE--
OI!, NOBODY DROWNED--
BECAUSE YOU SAVED THEM ALL!
YOU TWO SHOULD RELAX AND DO TEENAGER THINGS TOGETHER! I REMEMBER THOSE DAYS--
IMO, YOU ALWAYS TALK ABOUT HOW YOU ALREADY HAD THREE JOBS WHEN YOU WERE EIGHTEEN!
EXACTLY! I SHOULD HAVE HAD MORE, BUT I WAS TRYING TO TAKE IT EASY.
I HAVE TO GO WORK ON SOME NEW DESIGNS FOR THE BOUTIQUE. BEN, PLEASE MAKE SURE SUMMER DOESN'T DROWN IN THE POOL!
I CAN SWIM!

OKAY, FOR REAL. I KNOW SUMMER HAS HER PIE CHARTS, BUT HOW IS BEN NOT HER SECRET ADMIRER?! HE'S CLEARLY ADMIRING... **EVERYTHING.**
WE SHOULD DEFINITELY BE LOOKING FOR HIS NAME IN THE RECEIPTS!

SO...
SO...

UM, THESE ARE MY FRIENDS! CHER, DIONNE, AND TAI! DIONNE'S PLANNING A PARTY AND I--I'M SUPPOSED TO BE HELPING HER TASTE THESE CAKES!
I SHOULD GET BACK TO MY ***MULTI-TASKING!***

LET ME HELP.

OH, YOU'VE GOT A LITTLE FROSTING...

MMM, THIS IS FROM CANDY'S CAKERY, RIGHT? MY FAVE! I'D RECOGNIZE THAT PERFECT ANGEL FOOD SPONGE ACTION ANYWHERE! AND THAT FROSTING-- LIKE A CLOUD...

SO, YOU DIG ON THAT FROSTING, EH? LIKE...YOU REALLY LIKE IT?
YES...?
BUT DO YOU ALSO LIKE... CONFETTI?!

I...GUESS? I HAVEN'T REALLY THOUGHT ABOUT--
A-HA, SO YOU ADMIT IT!
YOU LOOOOOVE CONFETTI! CONFETTI IS, LIKE, YOUR TOTAL JAM!

WHERE WERE YOU TODAY AT 10:42 A.M.?!
AT THE BEACH? WORKING? HEY, DIDN'T I SEE YOU GUYS THERE, VISITING SUMMER--
SO YOU ADMIT THAT, TOO!

I'M GONNA GO SEE IF YOUR IMO NEEDS ANY HELP, SUMMER. TV LATER? I TAPED HOUSE OF STYLE.
SMACK
S-SURE.

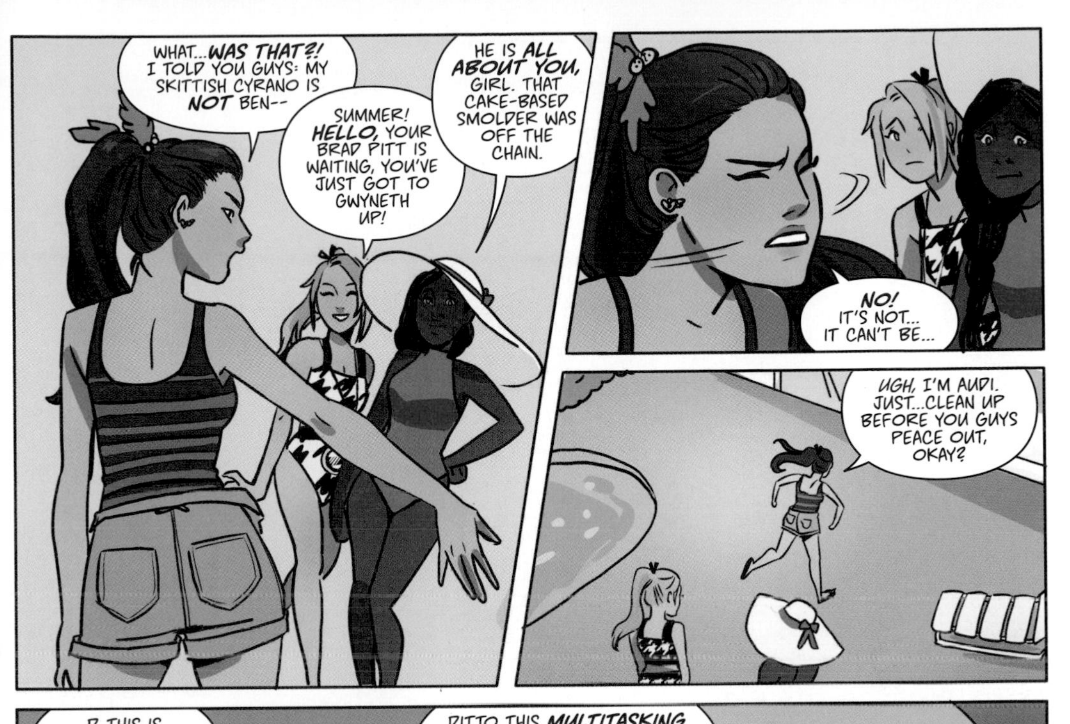
WHAT...**WAS THAT?!** I TOLD YOU GUYS: MY SKITTISH CYRANO IS **NOT** BEN--
SUMMER! **HELLO,** YOUR BRAD PITT IS WAITING, YOU'VE JUST GOT TO GWYNETH UP!
HE IS **ALL ABOUT YOU,** GIRL. THAT CAKE-BASED SMOLDER WAS OFF THE CHAIN.
NO! IT'S NOT... IT CAN'T BE...
UGH, I'M AUDI. JUST...CLEAN UP BEFORE YOU GUYS PEACE OUT, OKAY?

D, THIS IS **SO HEINOUS!** DETECTIVE CHER IS **FAILING** ON ALL FRONTS!
DITTO THIS **MULTITASKING MATTER!** IN ADDITION TO THE SUMMER DEBACLE, I DIDN'T GET THE LANTERNS, THE CONFETTI CLUE SEEMS TO BE A BUST, AND WE'RE STILL NOT DONE WITH THE FAVORS--
UM, GUYS?

I THINK I MESSED UP ON THE MULTITASKING TIP.

Flowers by François
IN THE FACE OF MOUNTING CATASTROPHE, CHER AND I AGREED TO DIVIDE AND CONQUER...ER, COMBINE OUR POWERS AND...CONQUER? WHATEVER. THE POINT IS, SHE AGREED TO STAY BEHIND AND CLEAN UP OUR MULTITASKING MESS WHILE I RUSHED OFF TO A TRÈS IMPORTANT RENDEZVOUS WITH MY BEACH BASH FLORIST EXTRAORDINAIRE, FRANÇOIS.
DESPITE THIS FLAMING DISASTER OF A DAY, I WAS DETERMINED TO CHECK AT LEAST ONE TASK OFF MY TO-DO LIST!
BONJOUR, FRANÇOIS! LET'S GET OUR BRAINS ATTUNED TO CREATIVE DESIGN CONCEPTS! I AM SO READY TO--

MURRAY?! WHAT ARE YOU DOING HERE?
SALUTATIONS, MY LOVE.

SINCE WE NEVER GOT TO GO TO LUNCH-- AND TALK-- I MADE ARRANGEMENTS TO BRING FINE CALORIC SUSTENANCE TO YOU.

WHERE'S FRANÇOIS?
I TOOK THE LIBERTY OF RENTING THE ENTIRE SHOP FROM HIM. YOU CAN MEET WITH HIM LATER--
LATER?! THERE IS NO LATER! I HAVE TOO MANY THINGS ON MY TO-DO LIST--
WE NEED TO TALK, D-- WE'RE ABOUT TO HAVE A WHOLE CONTINENT BETWEEN US--
I DON'T HAVE TIME TO DEAL WITH THIS--
OR YOU DON'T **WANT** TO DEAL WITH THIS--

GETTING THE BEACH BASH EXACTLY RIGHT IS IMPORTANT--
I THOUGHT **WE** WERE IMPORTANT--
MURRAY! I TOLD YOU! EVERY SECOND OF MY LIFE IS RULED BY MY LIST RIGHT NOW! YOU HAD NO RIGHT TO TOTALLY REARRANGE MY SCHEDULE JUST BECAUSE YOU WANT TO CORNER ME FOR SOME...***SOME STUPID ROMANTIC DINNER!***

MY APOLOGIES.

THERE'S ANOTHER SURPRISE FOR YOU IN THE BACK ROOM IF YOU FEEL LIKE PEEPIN' IT.
IF YOU EVER FIND SPACE FOR ME ON THAT LIST--LET ME KNOW.

OH...
SONG FOUR/SIDE ONE:
LISA LOEB--STAY
(I MISSED YOU)
D's Summer Mix!

NO TWO WAYS ABOUT IT--THIS DAY TOTALLY BLEW CHUNKS. SO I THOUGHT I'D HIT UP MY GIRL CHER FOR A LITTLE ICE CREAM-BASED COMMISERATION.
NOK NOK

HEY, D, I SEE YOU CAME PREPARED TO JOIN THE PITY PARTY!
PITY PARTY...? SUMMER, I THOUGHT YOU WERE MAD STEAMED AT US!
SORRY I WIGGED OUT EARLIER!

BEING AROUND BEN MAKES MY HEAD AND MY HEART AND MY... EVERYWHERE SPIN. I NEEDED TO TAKE A MAJOR CHILL PILL.
BUT THEN LATER, I FOUND ANOTHER NOTE SLIPPED INTO MY PURSE! I BROUGHT IT OVER, BUT CHER AND I HAVE BEEN UNABLE TO SUSS ANY CLUES.
SO WE DECIDED TO DROWN OUR SORROWS IN SUGAR--IT'S WHAT ALL GREAT DETECTIVES DO!
EVEN NANCY DREW?
ESPECIALLY NANCY DREW!

THEN BRING ON THE EXTREME LEVELS OF HIGH FRUCTOSE CORN SYRUP. 'CAUSE I'VE DEFINITELY ACQUIRED MY OWN SET OF SORROWS TO SHARE.

LATER.
WOW, D! THAT SOUNDS LIKE A **MAJORLY ROMANTICAL GESTURE!**
SERIOUS SWOON, GIRL.
YEAH, TOO BAD I'D ALREADY UNLEASHED MY **UNDILUTED RAGE VOLCANO** ALL OVER HIM. I'M JUST SO STRESSED AND I HAVE SO MUCH TO DO AND HE'D DISRUPTED MY PRODUCTIVE PLAN OF ACTION AND-- WELL. ANYWAY.

LET ME PEEP THIS NEW NOTE, SUMMER. I CAN'T FIX MY OWN LOVE CONUNDRUM, BUT MAYBE I CAN HELP WITH YOURS...
HMM...

SUMMER, I CRAVE YOUR BEAUTIFUL GAZE...
WHAT'S THIS...

FROSTING?!
=SNIFF=

AND NOT JUST ANY FROSTING. THE COMPLEX LAYERS OF THE SCENT PROFILE CLEARLY MARK THIS AS FROSTING FROM CANDY'S CAKERY!
BEN'S FAVORITE BAKERY!

NO...IT CAN'T BE... I MEAN...HIS NAME WASN'T IN THOSE RECEIPTS, RIGHT?
WE DIDN'T FIND ANY NAMES WE KNEW IN THE RECEIPTS! THAT CLUE WAS A TOTAL BUST...
THAT JUST MEANS HE GOT THE CONFETTI SOMEWHERE ELSE! SUMMER...

BEN IS YOUR SECRET ADMIRER!

UM, YOU DON'T SEEM SUPER JAZZED?

I DON'T GET IT! HE'S SUPER BABELY AND SO SWEET AND...AND...HE TAPES HOUSE OF STYLE FOR YOU! PLUS, YOU'RE CLEARLY ALREADY IN LOVE WITH HIM...
EXACTLY...

...I'M ALREADY IN LOVE WITH HIM.

I AM SO TOTALLY LOST.
WAIT...I THINK I COMPREHEND.
YOU'VE BEEN TRYING TO DENY IT'S BEN FROM THE START, WITH ALL YOUR PIE CHARTS AND STUFF. BECAUSE YOU KNOW THAT OUTCOME HAS THE MOST EMOTIONAL DEVASTATION POTENTIAL.
IF YOUR SECRET ADMIRER IS SOMEONE YOU ALREADY LOVE, IT OPENS YOU UP TO THE MAX LEVELS OF HURT. IT HAS THE POTENTIAL TO SEND YOU TO HEARTBREAK-VILLE.
SO YOU'VE AVOIDED THIS INEVITABLE CONCLUSION LIKE IT'S SOME KIND OF GROSS PLAGUE FROM OLDEY TIMEY TIMES. YOU'VE GONE OUT OF YOUR WAY TO AVOID IT BECAUSE YOU THINK THAT WILL PROTECT YOU FROM THE MAJOR SADS, BUT SUMMER--
--IT WON'T.

SO... WHAT DO I DO?
YEAH, D, WHAT DOES SHE DO?!
I...DON'T KNOW.
AND THAT'S WHEN I REALIZED--SUMMER AND I WERE TOTALLY WONDER TWIN POWERS ACTIVATE ON THIS FRONT. BECAUSE I'D ALSO BEEN TRYING TO AVOID HURT BY OBSESSING OVER MY TO-DO LIST AND DRIVING MULTIPLE METAPHORICAL FREEWAYS OUT OF MY WAY TO NOT TALK TO MURRAY. THE TRUTH WAS, I HAD NO IDEA HOW WE WERE GOING TO HANDLE OUR LONG-DISTANCE LOVE--OR IF IT COULD SURVIVE THE STRAIN OF AN INTERNATIONAL BORDER!
I COULD PLAN EVERY ELEMENT OF THE BEACH BASH...BUT I COULDN'T PLAN THAT.
AND IN JUST A FEW WEEKS, HE'D BE IN NOVA SCOTIA--AND I'D BE HERE. IN HEARTBREAKVILLE. POPULATION: ME!
SONG FIVE/SIDE ONE: EN VOGUE--DON'T LET GO
D's Summer Mix!

CHAPTER THREE

August

Tai Frasier
and the
Mystery of
The Heel's Needle

WELCOME, MISS EDWINA
Edwina Cleans House Mix!
—A Birkenstock Joint Orig
SONG ONE/SIDE ONE: THE CRAMPS--THE CRUSHER
WE
WHEN MY GREAT-AUNT ELLIE PASSED ON TO THE BIG APPLE FARM IN THE SKY, MY BESTIES CHER AND DIONNE--AND MYSELF, OF COURSE--SWORE A SOLEMN OATH TO MAKE SURE HER PARTNER, MISS EDWINA, ALWAYS HAD A HOME AWAY FROM HOME IN BEVERLY HILLS!
THIS SUMMER MARKED MISS EDWINA'S FIRST VISIT FROM OAK GLEN (AND THE FRASIER FAMILY APPLE FARM) AND I WANTED TO MAKE IT THE BESTEST VACAY EVS!
I HAD PLANNED, LIKE, A MILLION COOLIO THINGS FOR US TO DO...

RODEO DRIVE WAS THE **PRIMO STOP** ON OUR TOUR. PER CHER'S SUGGESTION, WE HIT ONLY THE MOST DOPE SHOPS...
MISS EDWINA, CHECK OUT THESE BITCHIN' CLOTHES!

BUT RETAIL THERAPY WASN'T REALLY MISS EDWINA'S JAM. LUCKILY, THERE WAS STILL PLENTY OF OTHER STUFF TO CHECK OUT IN THE BEV HILLS...

WE MADE A PIT STOP AT THE ULTRA-EXCLUSIVE BEVERLY HILLS BISTRO FOR SOME REFRESHMENTS...
WHERE'S MISS EDWINA?
WASN'T SHE GOING TO POWDER HER NOSE?
BUT THAT WAS MUCHO MINUTES AGO. OOH! SHOULD I GO SEE IF SHE'S BEEN KIDNAPPED?!

NO!
MISS EDWINA'S DISAPPEARANCE MIGHT BE THE BEGINNING OF A NEW MYSTERY--AND YOU KNOW I'M A MYSTERY-SOLVING MONSTER...

I'LL GO CHECK ON HER.

REST ROOMS
...AND THEN YOU PLACE THE APPLE SLICES IN A PINWHEEL...

REST ROOMS
...ON TOP OF THE TART FOR A NICER PRESENTATION...

ARE YOU A PATISSERIE CHEF BACK HOME IN OAK GLEN OR WHAT? YOU REALLY KNOW YOUR WAY AROUND DESSERTS.
REST ROOMS

OH, MY, NO! I'M JUST AN OLD APPLE FARMER WITH A FEW TRICKS UP HER SLEEVE.

SO MAYBE...ALL OF BEVERLY HILLS WASN'T REALLY MISS EDWINA'S JAM?
I WAS STRIKING OUT ON THE JAM FRONT. I WAS ABOUT TO BE JAM-LESS!

BUT A GIRL CAN'T JUST GIVE UP, SO ON DAY TWO, I TOOK MISS EDWINA TO THE L.A. ART MUSEUM, ONE OF MY FAVE SPOTS IN THE WHOLE CITY...

DIONNE HAD BEACH BASH PLANNING TO DO AND CHER LEFT A CRYPTIC CODED MESSAGE ON MY BEEPER. LOTS OF 1s AND 0s. WAS SHE TRYING TO SOLVE A TOTES NEFARIOUS **MATH MYSTERY?** ANYWAY, THEY WERE BOTH NO SHOWS FOR OUR ART EXCURSION.

THE STITCHER
...BUT I WASN'T SURE HOW HE AND MISS EDWINA WOULD GET ALONG, SINCE MY 'RENTS REFER TO HIM AS 'AN ACQUIRED TASTE.' AND I'D TOTES STRUCK OUT SO FAR IN SUSSING MY BELOVED G.A.'S JAMS!

Edwina Cleans House Mix!
SONG TWO/SIDE ONE: DIVORCE GUN-- MONKEY DANCE
—A Birkenstock Joint Original

THE STITCHER

WHAT?!
ARE YOU READY TO GET STITCHED!?!

WE ARE GONNA SEW THIS MATCH UP!?!
I LOVE THE STITCHER!
THE STITCHER TOTALLY RULEZ!

HUH. THAT ACTUALLY WENT...WELL?
WHAT'S A STITCHER...?

UM, THE STITCHER...? HE'S ONLY LIKE THE GREATEST HEEL IN ALL OF PRO WRESTLING!
WHAT'S A HEEL?

A HEEL IS THE BAD GUY IN PROFESSIONAL WRESTLING. HE'S USUALLY PRETTY FLAMBOYANT AND OVER THE TOP. IN OTHER WORDS, HE'S A REAL SCREAM TO WATCH. WAY MORE FUN THAN THE GOOD GUYS!
ONCE THE STITCHER GETS AN OPPONENT ON THEIR BACK, HE TAKES HIS INFAMOUS SEWING NEEDLE AND SEWS THE OTHER WRESTLER'S BODYSUIT TO THE MAT. IT'S BONKERS!
THE STITCHER IS DOING A HOUSE SHOW DOWNTOWN AT THE AZTEC THEATER TONIGHT. I KNOW SOME PEEPS WHO KNOW SOME PEEPS WHO COULD TOTALLY SCORE US TIX...I COULD SQUIRE YOU LADIES, IF YOU FELT LIKE DOING AN EXTRACURRICULAR TONIGHT?
AS MUCH AS THAT SOUNDS WONDERFUL, TRAVIS, WE ALREADY HAVE A DATE WITH TAI'S FRIENDS, CHER AND DIONNE, FOR A MAKEOVER SLEEPOVER THIS EVENING.

TAI-RANNOSAURUS REX, LOVE OF MY LIFE--WHAT SAY YOU TO RAIN-CHECKING THE SLEEPOVER MAKEOVER AND, INSTEAD, DOUBLE-DATING WITH ME AND MS. E FOR SOME PRIME TIME STITCHER ACTION?
WELL, I SUPPOSE CHER AND DIONNE WOULD BE DOWN FOR RAIN-CHECKING...
WHAT'S A GOOD-HEARTED NIECE-IN-LAW TO DO WHEN TWO OF HER MOST FAVE PEOPLE IN THE WHOLE WORLD WANT TO SEE A GROWN MAN IN A BODYSUIT DO A LITTLE SEWING?

SONG THREE/SIDE ONE: GLEN GOZA--RASSLIN
IT TURNS OUT THAT IT WASN'T, LIKE, ONE MATCH...BUT THREE. AND THEN THE MAIN EVENT: THE FINAL MATCH BETWEEN THE STITCHER AND HIS ARCH-GOOD-GUY-NEMESIS THE STERLING SMILE. I...DIDN'T REALLY GET ANY OF IT? BUT T LOOKED HAPPY AND MISS EDWINA WAS FINALLY JAMMING, SO I WAS DETERMINED TO HAVE A GOOD TIME.
GET THAT KID OUTTA THERE! HE'S GREEN!
WOO-HOO! STICK HIM TO THE MAT!
My BF took me to a wrestling match and all I got was this bangin' T-Shirt
I NEVER IN MY LIFE THOUGHT I'D GET TO HAVE A NIGHT LIKE THIS. IT'S AMAZING, TRAVIS. THANK YOU SO MUCH!

YEAH, SEEING A LIVE MATCH IS WAY MORE BOSS THAN SEEING A TELEVISED ONE! MY PLEASURE, MS. E.
AND THERE'S POPCORN AND HOT DOGS AND YOU CAN BRING YOUR OWN HOMEMADE SIGN--IT'S LIKE HEAVEN IN A WRESTLING RING. I MADE A LITTLE WRESTLING JOKE!

HAHAHAHAHA!
I THINK I'M GOING TO GO TO THE LADIES ROOM.
I JUST FELT SO TOTALLY...CLUELESS. MY CRANIAL WAVES COULDN'T SEEM TO BEAM THEMSELVES INTO THE WRESTLING HEADSPACE.

ARE WE... RRRRRRRREADY TO... RRRRRRHUMBA...?!
READY! READY! READY!

WELL, THAT'S A FIRST.

...BOO-HOO... BOO-HOO-HOO... BOO-HOO...

SWOOSH
...BOO-HOO-HOO...BOO-HOO...

...BOO-HOO-HOO...BOO-HOO... BOO-HOO-HOO...

EXCUSE ME, BUT IS EVERYTHING COPACETIC BACK HERE?

...BOO-HOO... BOO-HOO-HOO... BOO-HOO...

MR. THE STITCHER, SIR! NOT TRYING TO IMPOSE, BUT YOU SEEM REALLY UPSET-LIKE.

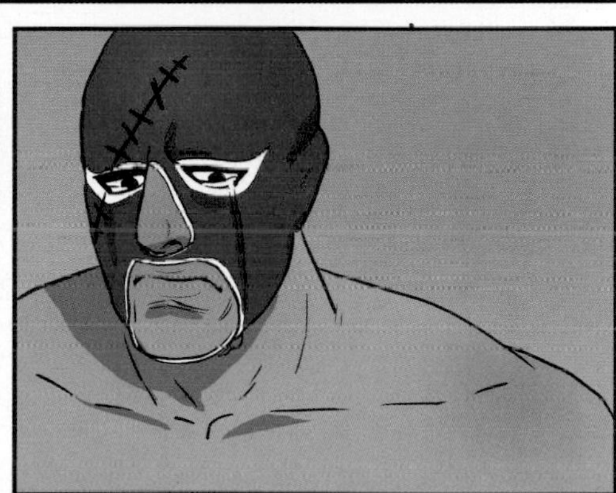

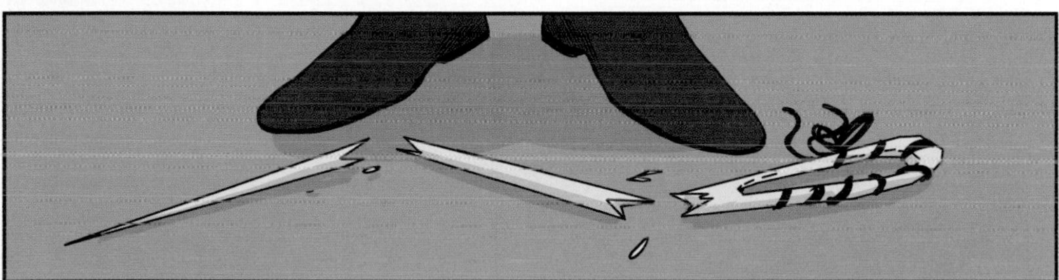

WHOA, THAT'S SO NOT COOL. YOUR KILLER NEEDLE IS TOTES BUSTED!

UM, WELL, MR. THE STITCHER, SIR--ON THE REAL, I MIGHT HAVE A FIX FOR YOUR NEEDLE.

I DON'T MEAN TO BRAG, BUT I AM AN ART SCHOOL FRESHER-IN-WAITING.
LET'S MOTOR.

BEING AN ARTIST, ONE MUST ALWAYS CARRY THE TOOLS OF ONE'S TRADE IN ONE'S BAG...
PACKING THE SUPER GLUE HEAT...
...DANGEROUS IN THE WRONG HANDS.
POP

(I'VE GLUED MY FINGERS TOGETHER MORE THAN ONCE AND IT IS NOT PRETTY!)
DRIP DRIP

AND NOW THE ULTIMATE TEST...
bangin'
T-Shirt
SHNK

RUMBLE IN THE AZTEC!
STITCHER! STITCHER! STITCHER!
WAIT...IS THAT...
...TAI-RANNOSAURUS REX?!
SO, I **TOTALLY GET** WRESTLING NOW.
NOTHING LIKE THAT MOMENT OF TRIUMPH... THAT FEELING OF TOTAL VICTORY!

AND FEELING **ALL OF THAT** ALONGSIDE THE PEEPS YOU LOVE MOST!
NOW THAT'S **MY** JAM.
YOU'RE THE BEST.
NO, **YOU** ARE.
NO, YOU ARE.
Edwina Cleans House Mix!
SONG FOUR/SIDE ONE: LIGHTNING BEAT-MAN--WRESTLING ROCK' N' ROLL GIRL
—A Birkenstock Joint Origin

I WAS MAD STOKED TO HAVE SOLVED MY SUMMER MYSTERY...BUT MY GIRLS WERE STILL IN THE DEPTHS OF THEIRS!
CHER? HOW ARE ALL OF YOUR INVESTIGATIONS GOING?
UGH, TAI! EVERYTHING'S A **TOTAL BUST!**

WAIT, DID WE JUST COMMUNICATE TELEPATHICALLY?! IS THIS A **NEW SKILL** IN MY DETECTIVE ARSENAL?
I DUNNO, GIRL, I WAS JUST TRYING TO THROW THE **VOICEOVER MOJO** BACK TO YOU...
WELL, THEN...

MY INVESTIGATIONS ARE SO TOTALLY BOGUS!

SORRY, GIRLS. BUT ON THE REAL: JOSH IS STILL ACTING WEIRD AND I'M STILL FIRED--
I THOUGHT YOU WERE GOING THROUGH A "TEMPORARY TRIAL SEPARATION"--
FIRED. AND SUMMER DOESN'T WANT TO CLAIM HER HUBBA HUBBA HUNKA MAN--
BECAUSE SUMMER ALREADY KNOWS IT'S A BAD IDEA.
I FEEL YOU, CHER. I HAVEN'T SPOKEN TO MURRAY IN WEEKS. I...I DON'T KNOW WHAT TO DO. THE BEACH BASH IS TOMORROW AND AFTER THAT, I MIGHT NEVER SEE HIM AGAIN!
OH, D! I WISH I COULD SOLVE THAT, TOO. BUT LET'S FACE IT...
I AM UNWORTHY OF THE ESTEEMED NANCY DREW MANTLE!
CHER HOROWITZ IS THE WORST DETECTIVE IN THE HISTORY OF EVER!
SMASH

JOSH...
CLICK
THAT...
THAT DOES IT! YOU KNOW WHAT? I'M OVER TRYING TO SOLVE THINGS THE OLD SCHOOL DETECTIVE WAY. I'M GOING TO SOLVE THINGS THE CHER HOROWITZ WAY!

For D & T! <3 C
SONG ONE/SIDE TWO:
SPICE GIRLS--WANNABE
MS. JENNINGS! MS. JENNINGS! OPEN UP!
NOK NOK NOK

MS. JENNINGS...?
WOOF!
MAGGIE? WHAT'S THE HAPS, GIRL?

creeeeaaak

MS. JENNINGS?
CLARE!

COME TO GLOAT, HAVE YOU?

N-NO--
I'M SUCH A FAILURE! ALL THOSE YEARS OF GIVING ADVICE AND ALL OF A SUDDEN...I HAD NOTHING LEFT TO GIVE! I WAS TAPPED OUT. THE WORDS, THEY WOULD NOT COME! I HAD TO RESORT TO BORROWING... OH, FINE, STEALING...FROM OTHER SOURCES!
I'M DONE FOR, CLARE! I CAN ADVICE NO MORE!

SO GO AHEAD AND LAUGH. EXPOSE ME FOR THE FRAUD I AM!
OH, MS. JENNINGS...

...THAT'S NOT WHY I'M HERE.

I DON'T EXPOSE PEOPLE--I HELP THEM. AND WHEN I STARTED LOOKING AT YOUR DILEMMA THROUGH A TRUE CHER HOROWITZ LENS, I REALIZED: YOU ARE TOTALLY HURTING.

YOU'RE NOT ADVICED OUT, YOU'RE BURNT OUT.
YOU'VE HELPED SO MANY PEOPLE OVER THE YEARS, AND NOW YOU NEED SOMEONE TO HELP YOU.

SO FOR MY FINAL TASK AS YOUR INTERN, I'VE BOOKED YOU A GLAMOROUS SELF-CARE VACAY TO THE BAHAMAS WHERE YOUR ONLY JOB WILL BE TO TOTALLY CHILLAX!
RECHARGE YOUR ADVICE-GIVING BATTERIES. THE WORDS WILL RETURN.
BUT...MY COLUMN--
Vacation Plans
--WILL FEATURE A VERY SPECIAL GUEST ADVICE-GIVER FOR THE WEEK-- MOI!
AND MY DOG--
UM, I'LL TAKE CARE OF HER! OF COURSE!
WOW. THANK YOU... CHER.
GET AWAY FROM HER!

I SAY, ANNE JENNINGS, I HAVE CRACKED THIS CASE AND KNOW YOU TO BE THE NEFARIOUS CULPRIT! DO UNHAND MY BELOVED THIS INSTANT OR--
JOSH!

WHAT ARE YOU DOING?! WHY ARE YOU DRESSED LIKE THAT? AND WHY ARE YOU SPEAKING BRITISH?

I--UH. I'M TRYING TO HELP YOU? SOLVE THE MYSTERY?
I'M, UH, DRESSED AS AVERY BARRINGTON, INTERNATIONAL CRIME-SOLVER EXTRAORDINAIRE. FROM MY FAVORITE SHOW, AVERY & ASTA. I'VE BEEN REWATCHING IT OBSESSIVELY TO PICK UP TIPS. SO I COULD ASSIST YOU IN YOUR WHOLE... NANCY DREW THING.

SO THAT'S WHAT YOU'VE BEEN ACTING ALL MAD SHADY ABOUT! BUT...WHY DIDN'T YOU JUST TELL ME WHAT YOU WERE DOING?

I WAS...EMBARRASSED. I HAVEN'T SHARED THIS SIDE OF MYSELF WITH YOU YET. THE SIDE THAT LOVES STUFFY BRITISH MYSTERY SHOWS. AND...I WASN'T SURE IF YOU'D LIKE IT.
I DON'T LIKE IT.

I *LOVE* IT.

DETECTIVE CHER HAS ALREADY CRACKED THIS CASE, THOUGH!
OF COURSE YOU HAVE.
Vacation Plans

SO, MR. SEXY BRITISH-SPEAKING GUY, WE MIGHT HAVE TO FIND ANOTHER MYSTERY TO SOLVE...
PIP PIP, CHEERIO! I CAN'T WAIT.

WITH MOST OF MY PRESSING INVESTIGATIONS WRAPPED, IT WAS TIME FOR DETECTIVE CHER TO FINALLY ENJOY SOME FUN IN THE SUN! THE NEXT DAY, WE ASSEMBLED FOR DIONNE'S END OF SUMMER BEACH BASH...
OH, D! THIS IS MORE INCREDIBLE THAN BARNEY'S TOP SECRET V.I.P. SAMPLE SALE...
IT IS, ISN'T IT?
BESTIES 4EVA/LAST SUMMER TOGETHER MIX!
For D & T! <3 C
SONG TWO/SIDE TWO: THE BREEDERS--SAINTS

IT'S FUNNY...WHEN I WAS PUTTING THE FINISHING TOUCHES ON THE DECORATIONS YESTERDAY, I HAD A **TOTAL EPIPHANY.** DIONNE DAVENPORT DOES **NOT** RESIDE IN THE NOT-SO-GREAT STATE OF DENIAL, WAITING FOR THINGS TO HAPPEN.
DIONNE DAVENPORT-- BALLER PARTY PLANNER, FIGHTER OF AGGRESSIVE KARAOKE GRANNIES, FUTURE WORLD LEADER-- **MAKES THINGS HAPPEN.**

AND YOU DECIDING TO HANDLE THINGS THE CHER HOROWITZ WAY INSPIRED ME TO HANDLE THINGS THE **DIONNE DAVENPORT WAY.**

MURRAY...

SO CHECK IT. I KNOW WE'LL BE AT LOCATIONAL ODDS THIS YEAR. AND I KNOW I CAN'T PLAN WHAT HAPPENS TO OUR POWER COUPLEDOM THE WAY I PLANNED THE BEACH BASH. BUT I LOVE YOU AND I WANT TO MAKE IT WORK AND...AND I NEVER GIVE UP, EVER. SO...

PLANE TICKETS?
FOR BOTH OF US--TO VISIT EACH OTHER. MULTIPLE TIMES.
AND I BOUGHT A WINTER COAT.

DO YOU...NOT LIKE IT?

I GOT YOU THE SAME THING.
I'M SORRY I KEPT AVOIDING THIS. I'M SORRY I AVOIDED YOU. I WAS...SCARED. OF WHAT MIGHT HAPPEN TO US.
BABY, I WENT TO THE DEEP VALLEY FOR YOU. WHAT'S A FEW THOUSAND MILES MORE?

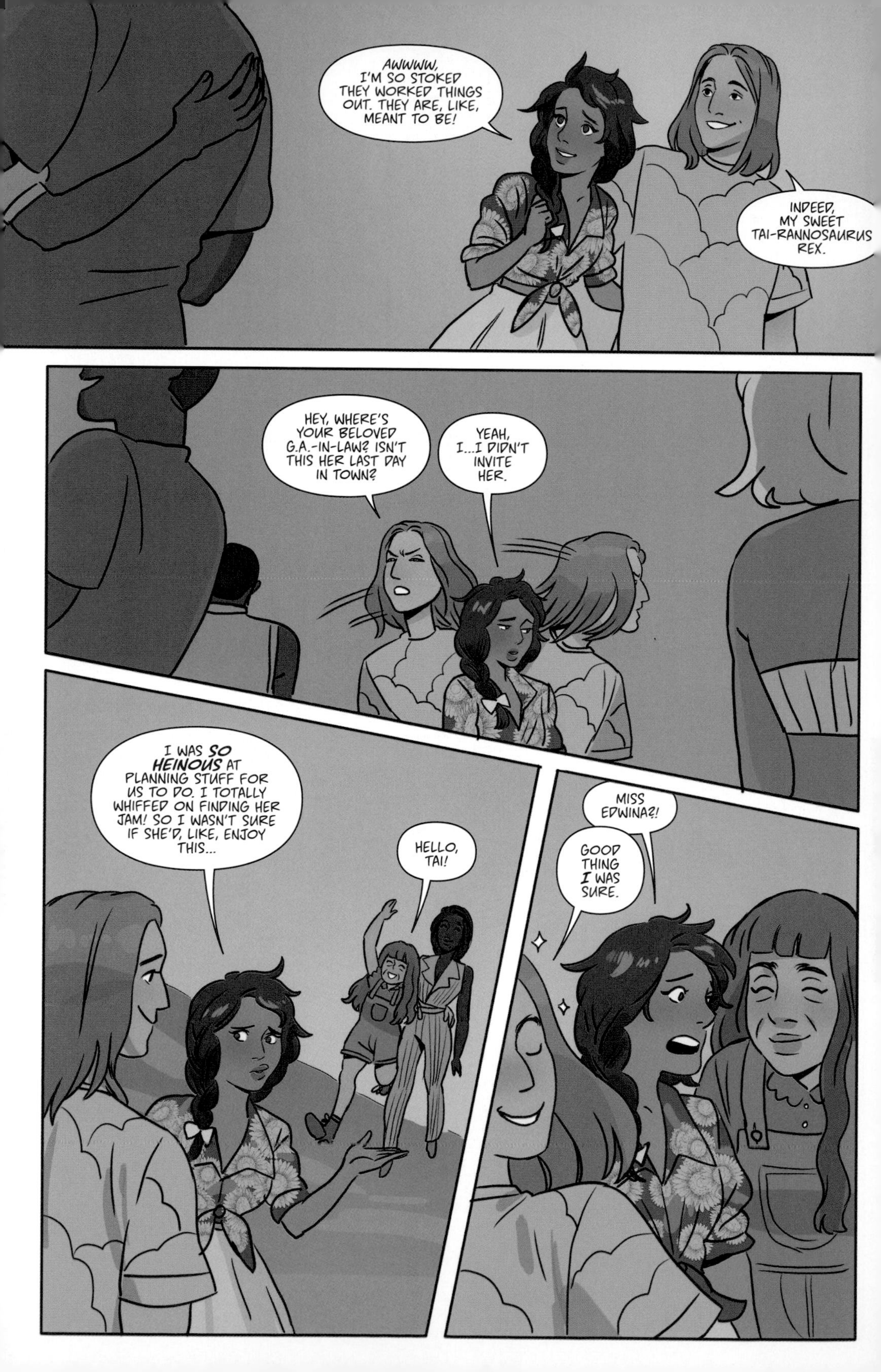
AWWWW, I'M SO STOKED THEY WORKED THINGS OUT. THEY ARE, LIKE, MEANT TO BE!
INDEED, MY SWEET TAI-RANNOSAURUS REX.
HEY, WHERE'S YOUR BELOVED G.A.-IN-LAW? ISN'T THIS HER LAST DAY IN TOWN?
YEAH, I...I DIDN'T INVITE HER.
I WAS SO HEINOUS AT PLANNING STUFF FOR US TO DO. I TOTALLY WHIFFED ON FINDING HER JAM! SO I WASN'T SURE IF SHE'D, LIKE, ENJOY THIS...
HELLO, TAI!
MISS EDWINA?!
GOOD THING I WAS SURE.

ALLOW ME TO INTRODUCE CLARA CAVANAUGH, THE ESTEEMED PASTRY CHEF AT BEVERLY HILLS BISTRO--THAT WONDERFUL LITTLE SPOT YOU TOOK ME TO ON MY FIRST DAY!
YOU...YOU LIKED THE BISTRO?

VERY MUCH.
YOU KNOW ME BETTER THAN YOU THINK, MY LAMB.

ALL THIS ROMANCE! SUPER INSPIRING, ISN'T IT, SUMMER?
I--

SUMMER-AH! LOOK WHO I BROUGHT TO YOUR BEACH BASH!
HEY, SUMMER.

BEN! DON'T YOU FEEL LIKE COMPLIMENTING SUMMER ON THE **BEAUTEOUS BEAUTY** OF HER SMILE?
UM...
ON HOW THERE ARE NO EXISTING WORDS IN THE ENGLISH LANGUAGE--
"BEAUTEOUS BEAUTY..."

?
WAIT A MINUTE! IMO! IT WAS YOU!
WHAT WAS ME?

YOU SENT THE SECRET ADMIRER LETTERS!
WAIT...YOU'VE BEEN GETTING LETTERS, TOO!?!

YOU SENT LETTERS TO **BOTH OF US?!**
THE TWO OF YOU REFUSED TO ACKNOWLEDGE YOUR **EXTREMELY OBVIOUS FEELINGS** FOR EACH OTHER! WHAT WAS I TO DO...

YOU...HAVE FEELINGS FOR ME?
OF COURSE. AND YOU... FOR ME?
ALWAYS.

THEN WHY HAVE WE NEVER--
I WAS SCARED. OF HOW MUCH IT COULD HURT IF--
UGH, ME TOO--
WANT TO BE SCARED... TOGETHER?

AND WITH THAT TOTES ROMANTIC, MOVIE CREDITS WORTHY SMOOCH, THE SUN SET ON OUR LAST SUMMER BEFORE ASCENDING TO THE COLLEGIAL PLANE.
NONE OF US KNEW EXACTLY WHAT NEW AND EXCITING SPINE-TINGLING MYSTERY AND ADVENTURE THE FUTURE MIGHT HOLD...
BUT FOR NOW? WE WERE GOING TO LIVE IN THE MOMENT AND STUFF.
NO "DUN DUN DUUUUUUNNNNN" NECESSARY.
SONG THREE/SIDE TWO: DJ JAZZY JEFF & THE FRESH PRINCE--SUMMERTIME
BESTIES 4EVA/LAST SUMMER TOGETHER MIX!
For D & T! <3 C
End

BEHIND THE SCENES

SCRIPT TO ART PROCESS

Script Page by Amber Benson + Sarah Kuhn

PAGE ONE:

(Splash Page)

MIDDLE OF THE PAGE: The Horowitz living room is packed with a ton of GIRLS (lots of diversity!) in PJs, running around. Including: THREE GIRLS stand by the giant projection screen television eating popcorn as an MTV music video plays on the screen. ONE GIRL does a cartwheel behind the couch while another GIRL cheers her on. We also see one lone cool boy, CHRISTIAN (from the movie), with a crowd of girls surrounding him. We see SUMMER sitting on a puffy armchair while AMBER sits on the arm painting Summer's toenails bright red…CHER, DIONNE and TAI (in matching pink PJs and wearing green clay face masks) sit in the middle of the room on the floor. Our ladies are like a calm oasis in the middle of a teenage girl-storm. Tai has a NOTEBOOK and a PENCIL in her hands. She is mid-writing.

TOP LEFT CORNER – an old Memorex tape cassette with flowing cursive writing on it.

1. MIX TAPE TITLE (handwritten): BESTIES 4EVA/LAST SUMMER TOGETHER MIX!

2. At the bottom of the tape (handwritten): For D & T! <3 C

3. CAPTION: *Song One/Side One:* ***MONTELL JORDAN – THIS IS HOW WE DO IT***

4. CAPTION/CHER VOICEOVER: *This might look like a typical Graduation Slumber Party…* **but it wasn't**.

5. TAI: --and name two hot guys.

6. DIONNE: That we, like, ***personally*** know…? 'Cause now that we've graduated, I am so over the ***boys*** from high school.

7. CHER: My dad's law firm totally represents Luke Perry ***and*** Will Smith… so that's almost exactly like we grew up with them! Totally counts.

At the TOP RIGHT CORNER:

8. CAPTION/CHER: *Dun dun* **duuuuuunnnnn!**

At the BOTTOM LEFT CORNER:

9. CAPTION/CHER VOICEOVER: *I mean…it* **was** *a Graduation Slumber Party. Duh. Like, it was totally the eve of graduation and the ex-senior class of Bronson Alcott High was totally having a seriously major hang at Chez Cher Horowitz. But it was also something* **more.**

At the BOTTOM RIGHT CORNER:

10. CAPTION/CHER VOICEOVER: *It was the beginning of what would prove to be a summer of spine-tingling mystery, swoony romance, and grand adventure for me and my bf Josh (and D and Tai and our friend Summer, too)!*

11. CAPTION/CHER VOICEOVER: *Okay, maybe now is a better time for me to say…dun dun* **duuuuu-uuuuuuu!**

Pencil Page by Siobhan Keenan

Ink Page by Siobhan Keenan

Colors by Cathy Le

Script Page by Amber Benson + Sarah Kuhn

PAGE FORTY-SIX (three panels)

Panel One

Dionne glares at her beeper. Cher, Summer, and Tai goggle at her.

1. DIONNE: ***Murray!*** That boy is trippin'. I told him my to-do list was going to keep me tied up for the rest of the day!

Panel Two

Dionne tosses the beeper aside and gestures to the rest of the girls.

2. DIONNE: ***Go, go, go!*** I have an hour budgeted to complete all of these tasks! Then I need to go meet with Francois and try to find another reputable source for paper lanterns…

Panel Three (maybe big panel to really sell the chaos here)

A flurry of activity as the girls all get to work! They all attempt this multitasking madness in their own ways: Tai is already getting things mixed up and eating the candies while trying to "read" her cake fork. Cher is focusing on every task with laser-like determination. Summer is getting creative, trying to hold the receipts and cake fork in the same hand while assembling the favor with the other. Dionne is going by her system, of course.

AT THE BOTTOM OF THE PAGE – an old Memorex tape cassette with flowing cursive writing on it.

3. MIX TAPE TITLE (handwritten): *D's Summer Mix!*

4. CAPTION: *Song Three/Side One:* ***Queen Latifah – U.N.I.T.Y.***

Pencil Page by Siobhan Keenan

Ink Page by Siobhan Keenan

Colors by Cathy Le

DISCOVER
ALL THE HITS

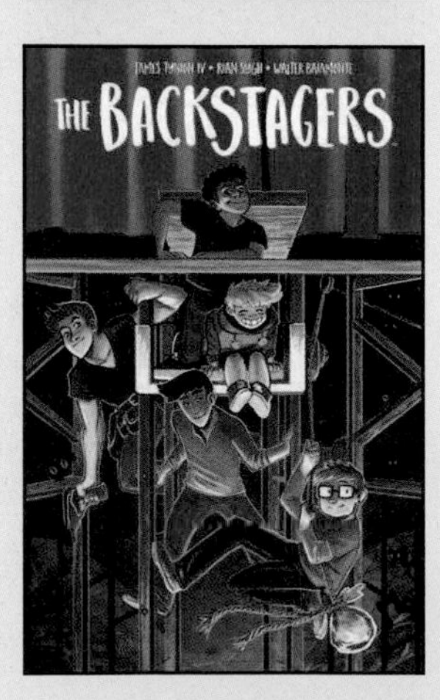

Lumberjanes
Noelle Stevenson, Shannon Watters, Grace Ellis, Brooklyn Allen, and Others
Volume 1: Beware the Kitten Holy
ISBN: 978-1-60886-687-8 | $14.99 US
Volume 2: Friendship to the Max
ISBN: 978-1-60886-737-0 | $14.99 US
Volume 3: A Terrible Plan
ISBN: 978-1-60886-803-2 | $14.99 US
Volume 4: Out of Time
ISBN: 978-1-60886-860-5 | $14.99 US
Volume 5: Band Together
ISBN: 978-1-60886-919-0 | $14.99 US

Giant Days
John Allison, Lissa Treiman, Max Sarin
Volume 1
ISBN: 978-1-60886-789-9 | $9.99 US
Volume 2
ISBN: 978-1-60886-804-9 | $14.99 US
Volume 3
ISBN: 978-1-60886-851-3 | $14.99 US

Jonesy
Sam Humphries, Caitlin Rose Boyle
Volume 1
ISBN: 978-1-60886-883-4 | $9.99 US
Volume 2
ISBN: 978-1-60886-999-2 | $14.99 US

Slam!
Pamela Ribon, Veronica Fish, Brittany Peer
Volume 1
ISBN: 978-1-68415-004-5 | $14.99 US

Goldie Vance
Hope Larson, Brittney Williams
Volume 1
ISBN: 978-1-60886-898-8 | $9.99 US
Volume 2
ISBN: 978-1-60886-974-9 | $14.99 US

The Backstagers
James Tynion IV, Rian Sygh
Volume 1
ISBN: 978-1-60886-993-0 | $14.99 US

Tyson Hesse's Diesel: Ignition
Tyson Hesse
ISBN: 978-1-60886-907-7 | $14.99 US

Coady & The Creepies
Liz Prince, Amanda Kirk, Hannah Fisher
ISBN: 978-1-68415-029-8 | $14.99 US

BOOM! BOX™

AVAILABLE AT YOUR LOCAL COMICS SHOP AND BOOKSTORE
To find a comics shop in your area, call 1-888-266-4226
WWW.**BOOM-STUDIOS**.COM